Lady Golden Hand

Nix Whittaker

LADY
GOLDEN
HAND

Wyvern Mysteries
Nix Whittaker

Reshwity Publishers
www.reshwity.wixsite.com/publishing

Softcover, ISBN 978-0-473-46823-1
Epub, ISBN 978-0-473-46824-8

CHAPTER ONE

The copious blood running along the channels of the cobbled street was likely the reason for alarm amongst the locals. They crowded the entrance to the alley but didn't wander in despite their curious looks. Rayne paid more attention to her partner than to the blood or the crowds.

Larkin rubbed his face and asked her, "Is it human?" It surprised Rayne the ex-Bow Street Runner was so squeamish. This was no worse than one of her sister's experiments. Unlike those Rayne doubted the scene was about to spew gobs of viscera in a sudden explosion.

Whoever dumped the body had chopped it up into chunks no bigger than a large rat. The smaller pieces, she assumed, were dragged off by the pragmatic life forms of Brixstane. The pungent smell of the typical Londinium alley over-powered the coppery odour of freshly spilt blood.

It was early in the morning, so at least there weren't any flies yet. That didn't mean the offal hadn't drawn a crowd. She eyed the bystanders with caution. Two constables kept the bystanders back at the mouth of the alleyway who seemed reluctant to wander any closer to the remains. Death was not an unfamiliar sight here, but it wasn't every day someone took the time to mutilate the body afterward, so Rayne could understand the curiosity and fear.

Rayne crouched down, shifting her blue wool coat aside so it wouldn't trail in the tracks of blood. The killer hadn't bothered to strip the body, and there were shreds of clothes still wrapped around the rough shapes of a human jigsaw puzzle.

She rested her elbow on her knee as she leaned forward to inspect the evidence. "One human being. Two feet, two hands. No head, though," Rayne informed Larkin. When he didn't answer she glanced up at him. His skin sported a shade of mashed peas as he looked determinedly at the crowd with steel in his spine. Rayne hid her smile. Larkin would not appreciate being mocked. The last thing she wanted to do was offend her partner.

Metal glinted in the blood. Gold. Rayne shifted onto her toes and leaned over. Larkin grunted. Being bent over as she was, he wouldn't see her face, so she didn't hide her smile. He would start with a lecture soon. He always did when she did something he didn't agree with. She had her fair share of lectures throughout her life.

Using her metal prosthetic hand, Rayne fished the ring out of the blood. The muted sensors in her hand made the action bearable.

The senses resulted from the technology dragons had shared with the humans. She didn't know the details, only that it involved small crystals. After growing up with a rudimentary claw, the intricate brass hand was a work of art.

Wiping the blood away revealed the engraving of a dragon motif on the gold ring. Popular in wedding rings ever since the treaty had been signed and dragons started taking humans as their mates. This ring was delicate and made for a woman.

Rayne frowned at the clothes surrounding the mutilated flesh. The cloth was well-made, a tight weave and hard wearing. Not something a rich woman would wear. A poorer woman would have cheaper material, a richer woman would go with a more delicate cloth. One section had a torn pocket. A small velvet bag half was revealed by the damaged fabric. Perfect for a little memento like a ring. This was the clothing of a man. That was no guarantee of gender though. That thought had Rayne turning over parts of the body.

Larkin protested, "My Lady?"

Ignoring Larkin, she found what she was looking for and rose to her feet. She cleaned off her metal hand with a handkerchief pulled from a pocket in her coat. "What is it now, Larkin?"

"A lady like you shouldna' be touching the dead." His accent grew stronger when he worried. He had picked up her own haughty tones over the years they had worked together. Though she didn't think he was ashamed of his heritage but rather he was a good mimic.

"I'm hardly a lady." Certainly not after working for the Metropolitan Police Department for two years.

"Your father is a duke that makes you a lady," He insisted. To society, it wasn't enough she was born to nobility, they had disowned her even when her father hadn't.

Rayne paused in cleaning her hand and ran the handkerchief over the ring. The blood had concealed an engraving inside. Holding it up to the light of the dawn that cracked between two buildings, she read out loud, "To my Beloved Eleanor." Lowering her hand, she said more to herself than to Larkin, "Not his then."

"It's a he?" Larkin's mashed pea complexion had warmed marginally so she was unlikely to have to dodge his morning meal. Rayne studied him a little closer. Today he looked a little less dishevelled than usual as his blue coat was pressed and the elbow darned where it had gone threadbare over the last few years. She doubted he would appreciate a compliment, so she stuck to the case in hand.

"Yes, our victim is male. One of some wealth from his clothes but not a nobleman.

A poor man would have pawned the gold ring and the clothes weren't made for a labourer." She flicked out another one of her handkerchiefs with her free hand and nestled the ring inside. Slipping it into her pocket for safekeeping. Rayne used the soiled handkerchief to finish cleaning off her mechanical hand.

Made from brass, her hand was articulated to allow movement but also to hide the gears and workings underneath. It made it difficult to get the blood out of the creases of each segment. Rayne kept flexing the fingers to make sure she hadn't missed anything.

Larkin asked, "Why aren't you out doing what other ladies do?" Ah, the lecture. She'd hoped he would forget his earlier objection.

Rayne focused on the task at hand with more determination than was strictly needed. Larkin was going for an old tried-and-true tirade. He saw it as his duty to help her go back to her 'place in society'. Every time he asked, she had a new answer for him. She hoped one day he would figure out all the reasons added up as concrete logic for her choices. Especially for why she was here as a constable rather than dancing attendance on other nobles.

"I have a brain; Larkin and I like to use it. Drinking tepid tea and eating stale cakes is not something I consider worthy of my time — or my mind."

Larkin snorted. "There are other ways to use your mind, Ma'am, you could have become a teacher."

Rayne held up her now clean metal hand. "I'd scare the little urchins witless with this." The hand was the main reason she had to forge a new path for herself in the first place. A mutilated woman wasn't accepted easily into society and certainly not acceptable as a match for the darlings otherwise known as gentlemen. Unfortunately, the main objective of nobles was to make the right match. That future was not in her cards. Instead, she found her own path and one she was pleased to be on. Even if it meant cleaning blood off her hand in a back alley in the greater Londinium area.

CHAPTER TWO

Rayne approached her workplace from the Whitehall entrance. She preferred the front entrance which was quieter than the one which opened onto Scotland Yard. There were other constables in the office areas and others like Larkin, who were the muscle for the department, milled around waiting for an assignment. Most had come from Watchmen positions or Bow Street. Now they all were Robert Peeler's vision and often called Bobbies or Peelers.

As the only woman who worked there as an investigator, Rayne garnered looks from visitors. Many were speculative but most were downright hostile. When Rayne had first come to work here two years ago, she had shamelessly used her connections as the daughter of a duke to bludgeon a position for herself amongst her fellow officers.

Making her way to Maynes' office to report back on the case he had assigned them, she ignored the tension from the others. Larkin went off to talk with the other constables. They wouldn't share titbits about the city while she was around, so her job was to talk with one of the leaders of the Metropolitan police while Larkin gathered gossip from the other constables.

Rayne backed up when she came around the corner and ran into Fields. A solid man, he towered over her much shorter frame. His own blue uniform was immaculate. Even the brass buttons were polished so she could see her own reflection in them. He had a leather brace for his two guns, which were far from the standard, of a single flintlock. She was also sure he had other weapons hidden from a cursory view.

He narrowed his eyes as he looked down at her. She salved her pride by telling herself he would have to look down on all his officers as he was well over six feet tall and loomed over her mediocre height. "Miss Ancaster? What brings you here? Your office is on the top floor."

Fields was technically her boss though they didn't interact at all on any given day. He had Maynes deal with her instead or went through Larkin.

Rayne tried not to hold it against him that he had voted against her placement at the service. But he had been outranked by her godfather, Sir Charles Rowan. Fields showed his displeasure in small ways. Mostly by ignoring her.

She cleared her throat. "Just reporting in, Sir."

"On that dismembered body that was reported? Human?" his voice speculative.

"Yes, Sir. Male." She clasped her hands behind her back more to stop fidgeting than to show respect.

"I was so sure it was a hoax." Fields waved her off. Rayne didn't wait to see if he wanted his own update on their case and dashed past him to Maynes' office.

Maynes looked up from the small desk perched in the centre of the room. Filing cabinets lined the walls and obscured a single window. There were no personal items in the room. Rayne had once heard Maynes' state that his life was his work. The evidence was this room which Maynes rarely left.

Maynes frowned. "Ancaster?"

She took a deep breath to calm herself after her brush with Fields and said, "I'm reporting in, sir." When Maynes merely stared at her she added, "The mutilated body found in Brixstane."

Enlightenment brightened his eyes. "Oh yes. Was it human?" He filled his pen from the inkwell ready to take notes.

"Yes, male, missing his head and some smaller pieces though I assume the rats got those. The head was deliberately taken." The head would have been too heavy for the rats to scavenge. Whether it was the murderer or some opportunist who wanted a trophy was still unknown. Rayne played with the brass button on the wool coat over her uniform. It was specially made for her as she was the only woman in the force. A little flattery with the tailor had gone a long way to gaining her the uniform.

"Head? Interesting. Any evidence?" He wiped off the end of his fountain pen when it left a splotch on the page and went back to taking notes.

"There was a wedding ring." She described it, including the inscription.

"So, he was married." He might have been. Most likely a widower if the ring came to him honestly. Or he could be a thief and stole the ring. Or the ring belonged to his long dead mother. It broke her heart to think he could have possibly been on his way to marry his sweetheart. The possibilities were endless. She didn't correct Maynes as he shouldn't have made that assumption even if the victim had been wearing the ring instead of having it tucked away in a pocket.

His pen scratched as it crossed the page. His notes tiny and neat. Her father's secretary would have been impressed. Most of Maynes' men couldn't read or write so Maynes usually kept the case notes. She had offered to write up the notes for her own cases but Maynes had his own way of keeping notes.

Rayne wondered if he did not approve of her. He was partners in running the place with her godfather and she didn't know what influence Sir Rowan had brought to bear on the barrister that Maynes had accepted her. Rayne didn't like to look too closely on how she had gotten her position here at the metropolitan police force. She was determined to prove she deserved that position though.

His voice brought her from her thoughts. "Anything else of note?"

"No, sir." If Maynes ignored the significance of a woman's name on a wedding ring held by a man she wouldn't mention it. It was rare she was given a case of any significance. She only landed this one because everyone thought it was a prank pulled by some bored children.

Maynes hummed. "We'll keep it open for the moment but without any name or clue to his identity I doubt there is much you can do to close this case. Good work. Have the Collectors taken his body in?"

"Yes, what was left of him, sir?" She didn't envy the Collectors their work. Though it was a promotion over collecting human waste from the streets.

"Fine, you can leave now." He didn't even look up from his notes. Rayne sighed as she left. Though she had fought her way to have a place in this organisation she had never managed to be comfortable with her superiors. She was afraid they would see her for what she was.

Defective.

When she returned to her desk, she scowled down at her flintlock taken out of its case in her desk drawer and laid precisely on her desk. There was also an assortment of polishing clothes pedantically placed to the side. Not one of them had been applied to the flintlock but it was a clear sign Fields thought she had been neglecting her weapon.

It wasn't like she carried it. Flintlocks were notorious for their inaccuracy and if Rayne needed her gun to deal with a situation, she was in a lot more trouble than a single bullet could solve.

A glance at Larkin's desk showed Fields had singled her out for the passive aggressive rebuke. Instead of arguing with her superior she sat down and started on her neglected weapon. While she was at it, she could go over her hand with the polishing cloth. She had been neglecting that as well and the buff to get off the blood had only shown how much in need it was of a good clean.

CHAPTER THREE

Rayne handed the footman her hat and her single glove. She had tried gloves with her mechanical hand but the material always caught in the articulated segments and restricted her movement and ruined them. Tired of the reproach from her maid she had decided it wasn't worth it, besides it was a social nicety and she didn't particularly care what society thought of her mechanical hand.

Duchess Ancaster, in all her glory, bounced down the stairs. Entirely too energetic for a fifty-year-old woman. "Perfect, you're home in time to be ready for the Inverness ball."

Lady Inverness was a close friend of the family and always made a point to invite Rayne whenever she hosted an event. Her events were always well attended despite inviting a lower-class element, as the high echelons of society saw it. It was likely the only ball Rayne would be invited to for the whole season.

Rayne groaned. "Do I have to go?"

Her mother waved a scolding hand her way. "You sound juvenile, dear. You'll never entice a young gentleman with that attitude."

Not that her mother was delusional, instead she saw Rayne for who she really was. Instead of for the deformity that blinded those in society, who focused on what she didn't have instead of who she was inside. No one would see her as desirable.

"Mother, you know I won't marry." Rayne waved her mechanical hand indicating the main objection men had to matrimony with her that no title or money could overcome.

"Pfft, any man who is intimidated by a little metal doesn't deserve to be in the family." Her parents had married for compatibility and that suited them well as it had developed into love. Her mother wanted that for all her children. Unusual in a society that married children off to others to cement deals and to create alliances all in order to shore up their failing funds. Her own investments already overwhelmed most gentlemen's incomes, so she didn't need anyone to take care of her.

Rayne tried to deflect her mother's attention. "You have other children to torture, surely you can find one of them to drag with you tonight."

"Oh, I've already dragooned your brother," shamelessly Duchess Ancaster admitted.

Talk of her brother brought a look of guilt to her mother's eyes. Rayne reached out, placing her hand on her arm and said, "It wasn't your fault." She knew what her mother thought. It was because of her brother that Rayne had lost her hand. A silly accident but her mother blamed herself as she had only produced one male heir out of the seven children she had borne.

That meant they had taken extra care with her brother's health. Including a reckless carriage ride in the middle of winter to get the family to the doctor because her brother had a fever. Unfortunately, the carriage had skidded on ice and rolled in a ditch. Rayne had lost her hand and from then on, her future had changed at the ripe old age of nine.

"Fine, I'll go tonight." She capitulated as one thing was still true; she loved her mother.

Lady Ancaster brightened suspiciously fast. "I'll have the maid put out your gold gown."

Rayne groaned. "Not the gold one. It shows too much flesh. Seriously, Mother, I'm not going tonight to be ogled by men looking for a mistress."

Her mother slapped her shoulder. "Never. You're a duke's daughter, no one would insult your father like that. Besides there is going to be a dragon there tonight and gold is appropriate." The dragons in the Wyvern Empire were all gold. Everyone at the ball tonight would be wearing gold in a hope to attract the attention of the dragon. It was the greatest achievement for a noble woman to marry a dragon. Unfortunately, no dragon lived in Londinium so the dragon would be in demand.

"Not gold, Mum. I'll wear that black brocade number I ordered last month." Her mother wrinkled her nose. The gown had gold accents but the black was more dominant. Rayne had ordered it after a spiteful woman had called her a lover of death. She hadn't had the opportunity to wear it as she avoided society when she could. Or to be more accurate society avoided her.

Her mother gave in too easily. "Fine, as long as you come with me to tea at Lady Pembroke's next week." Any hint of the pain before was gone from her mother's eyes. Rayne really shouldn't let her mother manipulate her.

"Mother, you're a shark. I think I'm bleeding." She put her hand over her heart, imitating a fatal wound.

Duchess Ancaster huffed at the play acting. "Oh, stop being so dramatic and go get dressed." She flapped a hand to indicate haste was needed.

Everett appeared at the top of the stairs. "You might as well give in, sis. She only gets worse if you resist."

Rayne skipped up the stairs and hugged Everett. He had been away at school for months and she had missed him. He was younger than her and it was through their games together that she had discovered her love for investigation. Back then it had been finding who had stolen his toy train.

He returned the hug a little too tightly. At least he wasn't embarrassed to show affection. There had been a few years there where he had resisted any show of fondness from her or others in the family.

His eyes looked sad when she pulled back. She frowned but he gave the slightest shake of his head so she wouldn't worry.

"Besides you have to attend in order to protect me." He shuddered dramatically. He clearly took after their mother.

Rayne patted his cheek. "You'll have to learn how to keep the mamas away someday. I'll take pity on you this one time. You'll owe me." Sauntering away she grinned to herself, she wouldn't have much time to ready herself for the ball, she was glad to have her brother home.

As she passed the small study on the second floor, she saw her sister, Katherine, curled up with a book absently chewing on an early meal. When Rayne called a greeting, she waved her hand with a slab of roast beef stuffed into some bread but her eyes never left her book. Rayne tutted at the scholarly bent that would have been beaten out of most women of society but encouraged in their family.

When Rayne arrived in her room, the maid was already laying out her black brocade which indicated her mother had planned all of this.

———

The Inverness ball was a shindig worthy of the name. Carriages lined the street as those who had timed it perfectly were able to alight without an interminable wait. Others had to entertain themselves while they waited. Footmen in red and gold helped them from their carriage when their time arrived to disembark.

Duchess Ancaster was a General when it came to timing. They arrived just before the crowds but still fashionably late. Their own wait had been minutes instead of hours.

Everett didn't wait for the footmen to help and skipped out of the carriage. He still had the lanky swagger of youth but he was filling out into a frame that had been too awkward and tall for his teenage self. He probably would need help to keep away marriage minded mothers after all. They were barely inside when Everett said as he brushed passed them, "See you later."

Duchess Ancaster huffed, exasperated by her son. "That boy." They watched him socialise with some men who were working on a bridge that would span the Thames in Westminster. The second bridge of its kind. Everett wasn't fascinated by bridges but he knew he could escape marriage minded mamas by hiding out with the dreadfully boring men who spoke only of their work. If any braved the scholars, then it was Rayne's job to play interference.

Together Rayne and her mother eyed the ball room. Duchess Ancaster announced, "A very mixed crowd."

Rayne snorted softly. "You mean there are people from every level of society? I would never have considered you a snob, mother."

"Not a snob but I would have worn a different dress." Probably one even more flamboyant than the emerald velvet and lace conflagration she currently wore. Duchess Ancaster liked to make a splash when she could.

She whacked Rayne on her arm with her fan and gestured with it to a space on the other side of the ballroom. "That dragon is here."

"You're surprised? You were the one who told me he would be here." Across the room stood the dragon. There was not much to discern him from normal men. He wasn't overly tall but he had striking features. Hair the colour of dusty mahogany.

It was his eyes that set him apart. They were as golden as a hundred-year-old whiskey. He was dressed in a red and gold tailed coat. The fashion was a little out of date but he was still a dashing figure. As evidenced by the tittering women who stood suspiciously close. The dragon didn't pay them any attention.

Instead, he seemed very involved in a conversation with another gentleman.

Duchess Ancaster said, "I see Lady Inverness. I'll give her our greetings. Don't go anywhere. I want you to meet the dragon."

Rayne couldn't help but comment sarcastically, "Will you obtain an introduction?" It was usual for matrons to introduce new people to each other to maintain propriety.

Duchess Ancaster whacked her with the fan again. "For a dragon? You have to be kidding. Dragons hate society and its airs. We'll just go up to him and introduce ourselves."

Duchess Ancaster sauntered off. Before Rayne could decide whether to wander off in search of some sustenance Sir Laurie said by her elbow, "Your Mother has certainly aged well. It runs in the family. A pity it skipped a generation, or could your true pedigree be showing."

Rayne could not be accused of not being fully armed. She raised a single eyebrow a fraction and sniffed in disdain. "Are you implying my father's pedigree isn't good enough or that my mother is dishonourable enough to cuckold my father?" She ignored the fact that he had just called her old. The best way to deal with these kinds of insults was never to let them slide. Acknowledge and disarm was her father's policy on insults in general.

"I would never imply that," he sneered. She didn't want to insult him or call him out as that would only escalate the situation, instead she raised an eyebrow. He had once been the Governor of Londinium and now he held a prominent position at a bank that dealt with many of the people here. They would step up to protect him against the defective daughter of a duke. Not even good enough to marry, so in their eyes useless to society.

When it was clear he was going to stand by the lie she flashed him her teeth in a mockery of a smile and said, "Excuse me, sir, I see my brother." She sauntered off without even trying to pretend she was looking for her brother and stopped when she was far enough, he wouldn't think of starting a conversation with her again.

Lady Beechworth sidled up to Rayne with a spare glass of punch. At least the woman offered a gift when she came to gossip. "Seen the dragon yet?"

"He has a name," Rayne corrected her though she didn't actually know it herself. Lady Beechworth was dressed in a deep blue that suited her skin tone. She was about the same age as Rayne's mother, though Lady Beechworth didn't use age to discriminate when it came to making friends. Instead, she gathered around her the most interesting people in society. She claimed they had the best stories.

"Yes, but with so few dragons in England everyone is just calling him dragon." One thing about Lady Beechworth, she always said what was on her mind. There was no chance of sly insults. If Lady Beechworth didn't approve of someone, she would announce it to their face.

"I think that is all they care about. That he is a dragon." Rayne could imagine that he had been reduced to his components by the Ton. They could cut even with their compliments.

Lady Beechworth snorted as they watched the debutants simper close to the dragon, who spoke rapidly and emphatically with a harried lord. Dragons had never bothered to learn how to socialise with humans. Being the top of the food chain Rayne could understand the hierarchy of thought there. Dragons in general made people nervous even when they weren't reminded that dragons saw humans as an afternoon snack.

Lady Beechworth turned philosophical and she pondered out loud, "I wonder if the girls realise that in attempting to be just like other women chosen by dragons, they have actually taken themselves out of the running. The whole point of collecting is to gather things of a unique nature." She waved her glass of punch towards the gaggle of girls all in gold gowns. No doubt they could all sing, play the pianoforte and paint a decent water colour. At least having her destiny so drastically changed at a young age meant Rayne had skipped many of those pursuits.

She could sing but only passably and was pleased she didn't have to torture people with her mediocre renditions at insipid recitals.

Though it had been her left hand that had been amputated everyone had been sympathetic with any skill that required hands and when she had expressed a dislike for the pianoforte and painting, she had been released from learning what was now a pointless skill in her current career.

Lady Beechworth continued with her own musings. "You would in fact be more of an interest to the dragon. Your career as the only female police investigator at the Scotland Yard, and your hand, place you in a class of your own. You should try to get his attention. He'd make you an admirable catch."

"He isn't looking for a bride." It was important to make sure Lady Beechworth didn't start playing matchmaker. Duchess Ancaster was formidable enough. If the two ever combined their efforts Rayne wouldn't stand a chance.

"How do you know that?" Lady Beechworth's voice was suddenly sharp.

"He hasn't looked at any of the women." The dragon was in an emphatic conversation with a gentleman whose eyes were slowly glazing over. The women jostled, urging each other to approach the dragon but unwilling to break protocol.

"Hardly anyone here of an interest to him. Can't blame him for finding other entertainment. I'm sure if he met you, he would change his mind." Lady Beechworth was like a dog with a bone. She was unlikely to drop the subject unless Rayne convinced her to.

"I'm not looking for a groom either." The sharpness in her voice wasn't to be mistaken and Lady Beechworth tipped her head to the side to take in Rayne.

Eventually she came to a decision and tutted. "A shame. He could do with the companionship. Especially after the scandal that surrounded his first wife's death. He has been away from society and people for four years." Dragons were essentially immortal and any woman who married a dragon managed to benefit from that with an extended life span themselves. It was unusual for a dragon bride to die from disease or childbirth.

"How did she die?" Grateful for the new direction of the conversation, Rayne asked.

"Murder." More interesting and something which appealed to Rayne. Lady Beechworth at least was decent enough to continue with the whole story when she saw Rayne was mildly interested. "They had only been married for less than a week. A whirlwind romance. As it always is with dragons, they are an impatient lot for beings that are immortal. It was said she had changed her mind and ran away from him. He went searching throughout the city only to find someone had murdered her and left her to rot in the Thames. He was distraught and blamed himself. He left Londinium after that. I don't think he has returned since. Not sure what brought him back. I think Eleanor was silly to run away from that handsome dragon."

"Eleanor?" It was probably a coincidence she bore the same name that was engraved on the wedding ring. But what if what had brought the dragon to Londinium was the ring? Maybe he had killed the man with the ring. Except the dragon would have likely taken the ring if that was the case and disposed of the body in a more permanent way.

There were flaws in her theory but still intriguing enough for her to hand her empty punch glass to a passing footman. "I think I'll go and talk to the dragon after all." Lady Beechworth chuckled, seeing this as a victory.

Rayne approached the dragon and she bowed her head a little in greeting. "Lord Dragon," she said politely.

"It's Victor." He offered his name as his eyes flashed with gold interest. The lord, the dragon had been torturing with his chatter, muttered an excuse and made his escape.

Victor glanced after the man only briefly before he took her in. His eyes rested on her hand. He grabbed for it but she had known the acquisition-minded dragon would attempt the move, so it was easy to evade him.

"Tut, tut Dragon, it's rude to grab things." She wagged a finger of her normal hand as she would with a naughty child. He did not look embarrassed. Rayne didn't think the breed could feel shame.

He asked, excitement making him shift from foot to foot, "Is it made from brass? Do you have any sensation? Is it easy to maintain? I've heard of the progress in prosthetics but I haven't come across one yet. Fascinating."

"My father had a tinker from the continent brought over to make it for me a few years ago. Before that I had something a lot less sophisticated. I'm interested to know, dragon, why you have returned to Londinium? I heard you left years ago."

"Victor," he reminded her, "and I thought it was time. This is my territory anyway." He shrugged. His eyes still on her hand rather than on her face. She had caught people staring before but never this blatantly. Colour touched her cheeks. Coughing to cover her reaction she stayed on topic.

"Londinium is your territory?"

"Well, I have a place out in Surrey. Londinium, like most cities, is considered neutral though fighting amongst dragons is practically unheard of in the Empire. We are a family. I also have a place in town where I'm staying at the moment."

"Are you related to the Empress then?" Most of the nobility were related to the Empress but it was rumoured that the dragons had closer links.

He snorted at the concept. "Unlikely. I never knew my parents. The Emperor always kept tabs on his relatives, and he would have claimed me by now if I was related. No, I mean we have made a family. Are you sure I can't examine your hand closer?" She didn't correct him that it was an Empress on the throne. He must find it hard to keep up with the ruling monarch when they never remained long on the throne and he was so long lived.

"You may, but I have a few questions of my own." She offered her hand, which he took in his own with reverence instead of revulsion. He twisted and turned her hand gently, aware that it was still attached to her. There were many who treated it like it was an accessory instead of the extension of herself it was.

He pushed her sleeve up cautiously to reveal the edge of the mechanical hand. It was held on with leather straps that were then attached to a harness that went under her gown and across her torso. Unless someone cut the leather there was no way they could detach her hand. Considering the small fortune her father had paid for the hand it was of some comfort to know it couldn't be easily stolen.

He bent her fingers individually and peered between the creases to have a peek at the inner workings. While he was distracted, she asked, "Did you ever give your bride a wedding ring?"

"Of course. Dragons always share their collection with their brides. A delicate little thing. She never liked anything too fancy, so it was an engraved gold band." Awkwardly, as he still had her hand in his as he continued to look at the workmanship the plated brass revealed, she took the ring out of her pocket. She always insisted on pockets on her gowns. Reticules were too annoying to bear.

He let go of her hand to focus on her face. "Why are you asking?"

Glad he had released her hand as she needed it to fold back the handkerchief to reveal the ring. Rayne wasn't sure what reaction she had expected but the bright blue light had her stumbling back. His dragon form filled the space with golden scales. He crouched low, so he didn't damage the ceiling. His large square head had short horns on the top and threatened to gouge the plaster on the ceiling. She could make out the individual gold scales of his body as she backed up. His chest had finer scales that were pearlescent rather than gold while the rest of his body had scales the size of her palm.

He roared but Rayne managed to keep her feet though she did turn pale. His teeth were closer than was comfortable. And certainly larger than was comfortable.

His claws slammed down on either side of her. Hardwood floors shattered and showered her with splinters. She flinched as pain sliced her cheek. Hot breath bathed her as Victor roared. Saliva dripped off teeth that were as long as her arm.

His roaring stopped and he turned, his tail whipped people off their feet. Rayne could now hear people screaming and running. They shouldn't have bothered as Victor was heading away. Besides with the treaty in place he wasn't about to turn the ball into a buffet.

He disappeared and a flash of light outside revealed he had transported himself outside. She had never heard of dragons being able to do that. She knew they could manipulate matter and store things away but she hadn't been aware that they could transport themselves over space. She ran to the window and saw him flying over the city.

One thing was clear. The ring had belonged to his dead wife. Also, she was unlikely to be invited to Inverness' next ball.

Everett said behind her, "That was spectacular. Highly entertaining and you'll be the talk of society for a whole ten minutes.

Mother has gone for the carriage. If you want to get out of here without more talk, you need to move."

Rayne finally took in the carnage of the ballroom. It was almost deserted with people huddled in fear on the opposite side. There was a flurry of activity from the servants and the host who tried to calm down their guests. As Rayne passed the guests there was a whisper of 'lady golden hand.' She clenched her mechanical hand against the urge to hide her disfigurement.

Once in the carriage her mother said, "Well, that was spectacular." Everett grunted with agreement as he also joined them in the carriage. Duchess Ancaster seemed unaware she had echoed her son's sentiment on the whole fiasco though Rayne doubted her mother meant it the same way.

Rayne buried her face in her hands and said, "I'll never be able to live that down."

Everett snorted. "It only adds to your legend, Lady Golden Hand."

"Don't call me that." Rayne snapped.

"Why not? It suits you." Everett poked her prosthetic hand and she recoiled and glared at his juvenile teasing.

"It only focuses on my mutilation not on what I am capable of." The shocked silence in the carriage had her remembering their mother was present and she didn't appreciate the self-deprecating humour Rayne and her brother shared.

"Sorry," he said sufficiently contrite.

"You are not mutilated." But there was a brokenness to their mother's voice. If Rayne didn't know her mother had a core of steel, she would have thought her mother was truly affected. Instead, this was just her usual attempt to manipulate her strong-willed children into behaving. Rayne slumped back on the squibs and decided silence was the better part of valour.

When they got home, their mother hurried up to bed while Everett suggested, "Father's stash?" They made their way through the orangery to their father's office. The large desk was looking a little neglected as their father mostly worked from the much more comfortable couch than his desk.

There was one place clear of clutter and with a little pressure to one of the carved roses and a click it revealed a hidden compartment.

Everett lifted the lid and passed her a piece of chocolate wrapped in waxed paper. She sat down on her father's couch and unwrapped the small candy. Everett also flopped down next to her. Rayne asked as she eyed the chocolate and considered the best way to consume it.

"Do you think I'm an embarrassment to the family?" she asked honestly.

"Yes and no," he prevaricated.

"That isn't comforting." She peeled back the wrapper. The chocolate was shaped into a small rose.

"Others seem to be embarrassed by what you do, so in that way you are an embarrassment. The rest of us couldn't care less. It isn't like any of it is your fault."

"What about becoming a policewoman? That was my choice." There had been a whole slew of reproach from the society mothers when she had decided to have a career.

Everett was quiet as he thought when he spoke it wasn't what she had thought he was contemplating. "What made you do that? I mean there are so many jobs you could have picked. Dad would have supported you no matter what you decided to do."

Rayne shrugged one shoulder. The whole conversation was making her uncomfortable as she had to take an intimate look at her own motivations. Especially as her brother would want more than the answers she gave to Larkin. "I needed to be useful. So many of society are mere ornaments. When I became broken and useless in their eyes, it made me realise how useless it is to be an ornament. So, I wanted to give back more than my looks or my pedigree," she sneered the last, implying that she had no looks to be proud of in the first place.

Everett bumped her shoulder with his own. "You are appealing and don't ask me to say that again. It was hard enough the first time."

"What about you, Everett? Are you going to be an embarrassment?" This was asked with a much lighter touch. Her crisis of purpose had already passed and she was curious about the sadness she had seen in Everett's eyes earlier in the evening.

There was a smile in his voice as he said, "I think I might. I must think on it a little more. I don't know if I want to go back to school but I do know that I don't want what dad is doing." He waved to indicate their father's office. "This is so staid for me. I think I would die looking at all those numbers for the rest of my life."

"It fits him though. Just find something that fits you and don't care what others think." That truth had been hard won for herself but had given her a sense of completeness she wished everyone could figure out.

He licked the melted chocolate off his fingers, having already consumed his. "As long as I am not useless?"

"Yes. That is no fate for any of us. So, are you going to tell me what happened at school?" It was still a month till the end of the year. He was missing out on the exams so this was no casual visit. She assumed he had been kicked out once again. There was a long pause and she wondered if he would tell her. Since their conversation had been filled with hope rather than bitterness, she knew his future wasn't what troubled him.

"There is this girl. She is smarter than all the other boys and my professor wouldn't teach her." She must be pretty as well, as the wistful note in his voice was probably from a crush. "I thought I would show him. I went about it the wrong way."

"In what way? Wasn't she grateful? Oh, she yelled at you didn't she." She struggled to keep her laughter inside and made a coughing sound instead.

A sheepish look accompanied his reluctant answer, "Yes."

She mockingly sympathised with him in a singsong voice, "Oh, you poor baby."

"It was a stupid thing to do. I didn't help the girl and all I did was get a mark on my record and sent home early." He groaned dramatically. "They always threaten me with my record as if it will follow me everywhere. No one will see it once I leave school. The rumours will have a more lasting effect." Records. He was right about their penchant for writing everything down in their society. She wondered if there were any records about Eleanor's death.

CHAPTER FOUR

Fields stopped her by calling across the foyer, "Miss Ancaster, have you had a chance to see to your weapon?" His voice raised enough to cross the distance but also making it possible for everyone else in the office to hear.

Rayne crossed to Fields in the hope he would lower his voice. "Yes, I did, sir. Thank you for providing the cleaning cloths."

He sniffed. "It's a good weapon and should be treated with respect. Did your father provide it?"

"My mother, actually. She's the one who taught me to shoot." Her mother had grown up in the country and her father, who had no sons, had taken her along and taught her how to take care of the land. Which included protecting it from brigands and thieves.

"So you were trained by a woman. What kind of accuracy do you have?" His tone made it clear he thought her teacher was not qualified.

"I can hit what I want to if I'm within fifty feet or so but after that I'd be lucky to hit anything." He wrinkled his nose obviously not impressed with her honesty.

She shrugged and said, "It is the flintlock, sir. I'd rather have a rifle any day."

"Rifle? What kind of rifle? Some are much more superior than others." His tone changed to one of interest. Everyone knew the way to Fields was through the armoury.

"I haven't done much study but my mother got me a Hawken when she got me the flintlock. I much prefer that but I can hardly wander around Londinium with a Hawken on my arm." He grunted, begrudgingly agreeing. There were strict rules about which guns could be carried in the city. Most folk didn't have any access to weapons. The dragons didn't like them as they were one of the few weapons that could kill a dragon. Though that theory hadn't been tested as the invention of the gun had come after the signing of the treaty between dragons and humans.

Rayne shifted uncomfortably. There were several people watching avidly as it was unusual for Fields to engage her in a conversation.

They expected Fields to dress her down. That was the only time he ever bothered to single her out. He rubbed his chin thoughtfully and said, "You'll have to bring it in one day for me to inspect. Maybe rifles should be kept on the premises just in case." He waved his hand in dismissal and Rayne used it as permission to dash up the stairs to the archives and escape the speculative looks of the other investigators.

The archives were a small room at the top of the building. A single table in the middle was set aside to peruse the documents as they weren't to leave the room. The walls were filled with shelves and books. On the table was the book that would direct her to the different records. Rayne had barely opened the book that directed people around the archives when she was interrupted.

"What are you doing in here?" Maynes asked Rayne.

She looked up from the archived records and said, "I'm looking for the notes on an old case. I'm not sure if it is even here." Maynes pushed her aside to replace her at the cabinet.

"What case are you looking for?" His tone sharp. Rayne wanted to tell him she could find it herself if this was an inconvenience but Maynes so far was the only superior willing to work with her besides her godfather. If he refused to deal with her like Fields did, then she would be unlikely to be given any cases. Or relegated to nuisance cases. She knew the only reason her and Larkin had been given his particular case was because no one had actually believed it was a real body.

So, she bit her tongue and instead moderated her tone to a pleasant one and said, "The murder of a woman called Eleanor. She was the wife of the dragon, Victor."

Maynes' hands paused but he went unerringly through the files, as he said, "That was early days. Before even the police force. We have records on it as the Bow Street runners had notes on the cases we inherited. I remember it. I was a young barrister back then. Worked as a personal assistant for a politician. Messy business. They never found anyone guilty. Though I think the dragon did it personally. Vile creatures." He flicked through the folder and ran his finger down the reference list. He then went off further into the archives.

He spoke as he worked, "Any time you involve dragons, things get messy. I don't know why they don't leave us humans alone. I know the Empress is related to a dragon but that doesn't mean the rest of them have to stick their nose into government." He brought out a book and laid it on top of the table at the page noted in the catalogue.

"Make sure this doesn't leave the room." Maynes huffed in exasperation. Rayne could have found the file herself but pretending to need his help would prevent a conflict. Maynes would have been more upset if she had rejected his assistance. It confused her that people thought women were weaker when they insisted on doing everything for them in the first place. Rayne merely shook her head and picked up the book.

There wasn't much there, the names of the people involved and the address for the dragon which was helpful. She would see if she could interview him and find out if he could shed some light on it all. The ring obviously was his dead wife's and for the dead man to have it on him he would have been involved in the original murder. The clues weren't many but they did lead down a path she could follow. The interesting part was the name Sebastian. He was the man who was implicated for the murder but had been pardoned by the Governor. There had to be something there for politics to be involved in the outcome. Considering Maynes' attitude towards the dragon there might have been some evidence that was uncovered later that pointed towards Victor.

Larkin found her still in the archive. "There's a lady here to meet you." The emphasis on Lady meant it was not just a run-of-the-mill lady.

"A *lady*?" Ladies rarely entered the confines of Scotland Yard and when they did, it was to see people like Charles Rowan, her godfather and one of the leaders of the police force. They were never there to see her.

"Yeah, Lady Beechworth." Rayne quickly returned the file to the cabinet and went to the small office she shared with Larkin. Lady Beechworth looked at the newspapers framed on the wall. They were her most famous cases. The wall was pretty much empty except for the three newspaper articles.

Larkin's side of the office had more as he had served longer than her. She had taken the tradition from him. After working together for six months she bought him a stack of frames. It was from then that Larkin had accepted her as his partner instead of the annoying woman foisted onto him by his superiors.

Lady Beechworth spun to face her with her skirts flaring as she did. "A bit gory, this pastime of yours." Some gruesome sketches accompanied the articles. Entirely inaccurate but Rayne assumed it was to sell newspapers rather than to be informative.

"More than a bit gory. What brings you here, Lady Beechworth?" Rayne hoped it had nothing to do with the night before and the rigmarole that had happened at the ball.

"A bit of a scandal, actually. I thought I'd come to see you as you would know just how important it is to keep this all silent." Rayne motioned for Lady Beechworth to take a seat. She settled and smoothed her skirts nervously. This comforted Rayne as she recognised the movements of a typical female client. Rayne silently offered her a cup of tea. Lady Beechworth mumbled a thank you. She had almost finished the cup before she spoke again.

She didn't prevaricate at all. "You see, I'm being blackmailed." In the tone of telling her that the weather would be cloudy it left Rayne a little shocked.

"Blackmailed? Surely you haven't done anything of note." Lady Beechworth was her mother's age. She doubted she had the energy to get into the kind of trouble that would benefit a blackmailer.

Lady Beechworth waved it off and added, "A little youthful indiscretion. Unfortunately, this behaviour is tolerated in men but not in women. My girls are at an age where this could be very damaging. So, I hired a man to make inquiries. He uncovered an address. But now he refuses to do anything about it."

Lady Beechworth dug out a small scrap of paper from her reticule sitting on her lap. "Here is the address where the blackmailer lives." She reached over the desk with the slip of paper between two of her glove-covered fingers.

Rayne accepted the paper as she asked, "Why the caution on your investigator's part? He must be decent to have uncovered this."

"Apparently the man is an ex-police officer. The investigator is hesitant to step on any toes." The department had only been an entity for less than three years. For someone to first have a career as an officer and to lose that career meant he was probably notorious. She would ask Larkin later as he had been

41

working longer than her and actually spoke with the other investigators. She hadn't made friends amongst the others but it would be suicide to go after a former officer without finding out all she knew about the situation. If he was liked by the other officers and she arrested him, she would become a pariah amongst her colleagues. Well, more of a pariah.

Lady Beechworth knew her standing in the department was precarious. "But I'm bulletproof from scandal?" Rayne asked incredulous.

"Yes, your godfather is Charles Rowan. You can't be fired. So frankly dear, you are bulletproof." Her job, yes, but any relationship she might vaguely have with the other officers would die an early death.

Rayne smoothed out the note with the address under her hand and said, "I'll look into it."

Lady Beechworth beamed. "You are a dear."

Lady Beechworth had barely left when Fields entered with a large rifle.

He laid it on her table. "I heard your suspect is a dragon. You'll be needing this. Make sure you shoot him when he is in his human form. Hiding a dragon body is problematic with the treaty." How he had known she was going to question Victor was an amazing show of gossip in the department.

Maynes must have mentioned which file she was looking at and jumped to some conclusions based on the drama at the ball the other night.

Fields laid a case of shells on the table next to the gun. He nodded to her and left. Rayne was speechless. The gun was big enough to take down an elephant, the prey it was most likely made for.

Killing Victor would be more than problematic as she wasn't sure he was the right suspect. There were too many holes in any of her theories. Besides why would a dragon leave a body in the first place if he was the one who had murdered the mutilated man in the alleyway? Fields should have advocated for a trial but again that was also more than problematic. A human government daring to give judgement on a dragon would upset both the Empire and the dragons.

Larkin walked in and tested the rifle by lifting it up to his shoulder and closing an eye to imitate taking a shot. He returned it to the desk with a click of his tongue in admiration.

"A beauty. Is that one of Fields? He treats those like babies. He must have started to trust you if he is lending you one of his children." Rayne wasn't sure she this development in her relationship with Fields pleased her. She preferred it when he avoided her because of girl cooties or something else equally ridiculous.

She glared at Larkin who put up his hands up in defence. "I know that look. Rosie looks at me like that when I say something stupid."

"Rosie?"

Larkin blushed which was a sight to see. There was little that embarrassed Larkin. He shuffled his feet and admitted reluctantly, "My girl. She works in the shop on Masters."

"Good on you, Larkin. You deserve a good lady." She really meant it but it also jarred her version of the world. Larkin was her work partner and she had never seen him as a possible mate. For someone else to see him that way merely surprised her though it shouldn't.

Rayne reached for the rifle to put it away, using her metal hand. It ground with a screech that had her wincing in audible pain. Larkin tugged on his ear, pretending he hadn't been hurt by the sound. "Needs to be looked at, I think."

CHAPTER FIVE

Rayne found Everett occupied in his workshop. She leaned against the doorway to watch him work. The room was cluttered with the skeletons of a thousand projects that hung from the ceiling or sat gathering dust on shelves. Everett worked at a large table that was mostly clear except for his current project. It looked like a basket with a weird disk-shaped thing on top but shaped more like a screw that was flattened. Everett had his tongue sticking out the side of his mouth as he worked.

"Hey, Magamesa." Everett looked up at the old childhood nickname. One that Gregory had given him whenever he worked. It was a word from Africa that referred to his tongue sticking out like a cigar while he worked. He flashed her a grin before he went back to his work.

Rayne looked over his shoulder and asked, "What is it?"

"The flying thing that got me into trouble. It got a bit damaged when the teachers sent the students to take it down. I managed to get it back with the promise to never bring it to school again." She wondered if he had given that promise because he didn't think he would be going back either.

"Are you going back?" she asked, though she could probably guess the answer.

"I don't know," he answered distractedly, as he continued to work on his flying machine. Her brother was brilliant, for him to sound so dejected broke her a little.

Rayne put her metal hand in front of his face, forcing him to stop his repairs on the flying device. "I need some maintenance. It's making screeching noises." He motioned to a stool.

She rested her hand on the table and asked, "Do I have to take it off?" Pulling the stool closer with the tip of her toes, she took a seat.

"Let's see what's wrong first." To demonstrate she closed her fist and though it didn't screech it certainly made a grinding sound. "Sounds like some dirt has gotten in there. Yeah, I think you'll have to take it off." He motioned to the other end of the workroom where she could have some privacy behind a set of freestanding shelves.

Rayne plucked at her buttons behind the shelves and said, "The dragon would probably be interested in your flying device. My hand certainly fascinated him." She had to raise her voice a little to make sure he heard her on the other side of the room.

"He has probably seen better. It's just a toy." His voice was distracted, so he was likely finishing up with his flying machine.

"You shouldn't put yourself down. You make wonderful creations. Without you I'd have to send for Jasmine every time my hand gave me trouble. I would be weeks without it and I've had enough of claws and hooks to know how superior this hand is." Rayne unbuckled the straps holding on her hand once she had divested herself of her bodice. The hand came loose and left an imprint on the stump of her arm.

There were elaborate scars from the original injury that had turned silver over the years. They weren't even painful anymore though she could still remember it as a dull ache that never seemed to leave her bones. The hand was also superior in comfort. Her previous attachments had often rubbed her raw. They had left their own mark on her arm as well over time. Her mother had discovered an ointment that smoothed most of those away over the years she had the brass hand.

The doctor had only taken off the part where the bone had been shattered into tiny slivers and had left the whole part even though it wasn't pretty. It meant she still had her elbow which increased her agility. She placed her mechanical hand on a clear shelf and slipped her bodice back on. The buttons were difficult with one hand but for most of Rayne's life she had to deal with the lack of the limb. The buttons were also designed for ease of use. They were on the front as well, so that wasn't much of an issue.

She still wore her bobby uniform and it had originally been designed for men who didn't require others to dress them nearly as much as women did. Though the trend was leaning towards more practical outfits for women as time passed. She wouldn't be surprised to find outfits with pockets as the norm.

Once redressed she picked up her hand and came around the shelf. Everett had cleared off the table so he could work on her hand. "Do you think I could make a job of this?" he asked as he motioned for her to hand over her prosthesis.

"In a heartbeat. Is that what you're thinking?" He shrugged and she let it drop. He took her hand and carefully took off the shielding of articulated brass. Inside the 'bones' of the machine were made from steel and some crystals. Everett didn't touch those. Instead, he looked at the shielding first. He used a lantern to look inside and with a swab cleaned out the inside.

Everett scowled at the dirty swab and asked, "Is that blood?"

Almost definitely. She wasn't even sure if it came from the body they had investigated yesterday or another. "If I say yes, will you get mad?"

"No, disgusted. Why can't you use your other hand? That one is much easier to clean." He stuck out his tongue again as he went back to cleaning out the intricacies of her prosthetic.

"Yes, but it also can feel the blood. The sensory feedback on the metal isn't nearly as keen as my real flesh." He wrinkled his nose, probably at the prospect of touching a murdered man's innards. He must have felt the same as she did as he didn't bring it up again.

When he was finished, he put it all back together and handed it to her. "Check to make sure it is no longer screeching." She put on the hand without the brace. The ends connected with the parts embedded inside her flesh. Flexing her fingers, she moved the articulated plates with ease. Taking it off, she handed it back. "Looks good. Better yet, it sounds good."

Everett took it apart again, this time working on the innards of the hand. He dipped another swab into a jar of grease and worked it into the joints of the articulated parts. He cleaned out the innards of her hand with a lot more care than he had shown to the brass. This was the part none of them could replicate.

Everett said, "I wish I could make this."

"Some of your machines are close." He could make the articulated brass covering and even the steel structure inside. It was the augmented intelligence in the crystals, that made all this possible, that was beyond his ability. A technology taught by the dragons to humans who then applied it in ways the dragons had never imagined.

"Some but none of them could give the senses that you can from this. That is dragon magic." His voice wistful.

"It isn't magic, it's science." Rayne didn't like the worship of dragons. They weren't gods.

"It might as well be magic. They can manipulate the essence of the universe." He finished with the cleaning and handed it back to her. "Good as new. Now you can give society the finger without making a grinding noise as you do it."

"Har di har har," she replied as she took back her hand.

CHAPTER SIX

Rayne watched Larkin tug on the collar of his shirt. This was the fifth or sixth time he had done that. Glancing at him, she asked him, "A little too much starch?"

"First time for starch. I never bother with it." He didn't sound annoyed but rather bewildered.

"Rosie?" It was the only explanation for the change in his laundry routine and for the confused tone.

"Yes, she says my clothes need an upgrade. I was alright with replaced buttons and the pressing but I think I could do without the starch."

"But not without Rosie." His silence was significant. It was clear he wasn't used to the idea of having a significant other. Rayne also wondered if he had thought about his feelings at all beyond that he enjoyed being with her. It was amusing to watch him stumbling in new territory.

Larkin asked, "Are you sure we shouldn't have brought that rifle?"

The dragon had a place on Wilton Crescent. It was in a neighbourhood where they hired people to look after the exterior.

This was probably good foresight of the dragon who hadn't been in his Londinium home in over four years.

Rayne checked her appearance as subtly as possible but she shouldn't have bothered as Larkin was fighting his own clothes and didn't notice her discreet adjustments. If he saw her, he would probably rib her for vanity.

"I'm not going to meet a dragon with a gun that is the same size as me. Firstly, it will mean I won't get that conversation I wanted and secondly, I'll look weak, as if I needed the gun to face him. I'm not afraid of the dragon."

"Reports say he almost ate you the other night." Her hope that word had not trickled down to all levels of society went up in a flash of smoke.

"He reacted badly seeing the ring but there was no danger of him actually eating me." Rayne gave the door a sharp knock and stepped back to wait for the butler. The door opened on the dragon himself. He looked like someone had rolled him around on the carpet and the static had created his hair style.

His clothes were beyond rumpled as he mumbled, "What do you want?"

"Can we talk?" He eyed her up and down then looked at Larkin who stood a step behind her on her right.

"Brought muscle this time. Scared?" He leaned on the doorframe, most likely to remain upright.

"No, at the moment, you're just pathetic." He certainly was with his unkempt appearance and still in the clothes he had worn the night before.

"I appreciate being demeaned by a civil servant. It puts me in my place," he deadpanned.

Victor stepped back so they could enter. He rubbed his face, as he stumbled through the dim corridors, and she followed him. "I wasn't expecting visitors so I don't have anything to serve you. Unless you want some bourbon," he offered.

Rayne wrinkled her nose at the prospect. "I didn't think so."

Victor threw himself onto a dusty love seat. Or possibly fell. He didn't look entirely steady on his feet. He waved dismissively for them to take their own seats. Larkin wisely remained standing but Rayne politely accepted his offer. She dusted off most of the detritus with her mechanical hand as she didn't want to be able to feel the lingering grime. Still she sat on only the barest edge of the seat. Hands placed in perfect ladylike grace on her lap.

"I take it you haven't been in Londinium for a while." The rumours said at least four years but she would rather have confirmation. It certainly was suspicious that he had returned just as a body connected to his wife also was discovered in Londinium.

"A few years, I think. I left in a bit of a hurry, forgot to close up the house like I usually do." There was no guile in his voice so she assumed he had no better idea than the ton about how long he had been out of the city. Besides dragons were known to be cavalier with dates as they were so long lived, a year or two didn't make much difference either way. He eyed the state of his house with bewilderment. She wondered if he expected to be gone this long.

"You could hire servants," Rayne suggested, recognising the ploy for pity. Her mother tried the same but Victor was not as sophisticated as Lady Ancaster.

"Dragons don't hire servants we collect them." Rayne wasn't going to touch the issue of collections. They were quasi slavery, as far as she understood the whole relationship, with a touch of family thrown in. Instead, she brought out the ring again. Victor's eyes were drawn to the handkerchief.

He leaned closer to study the ring. "Is that blood?"

"Yes, we found it on a dead man's body yesterday. Are you willing to answer some questions?" Her prim sitting position only added to her professional air. She didn't want the dragon to become emotional, otherwise they might have a repeat of the night before.

The sitting room was already in a state. She didn't think it would survive the transformation of the dragon to his full size.

"Maybe. What is in it for me?" His eyes were now on her mechanical hand instead of the ring. It was true, dragons were fascinated with the unusual.

"How about a deal? You answer one of my questions and I'll answer one of yours." Interest flickered in his eyes, chasing away some of the liquored daze.

She asked first before he could start, knowing whoever started had the power in the conversation. "Is this Eleanor's ring, was she wearing it when she left?"

"Yes. It should have an engraving inside with her name. It was especially made for her. There aren't any others like it. How did you lose the hand?"

"It was a carriage accident when I was about nine. It was the middle of winter and my brother was sick. We were rushing to see a doctor when the carriage lost control and we tipped over. We were thrown about and my hand got trapped. It was crushed. They had to amputate or risk gangrene. Why did Eleanor leave you?"

"We weren't a good match. I made a mistake. So, she left." She raised an eyebrow. He was keeping things from her or outright lying. Even the lie told her something. He was embarrassed by the reason she left. There was little that could shame a dragon but getting it wrong with their mate was one of them. So, she let it slide.

He asked, "Who made your hand?"

"Jasmine Cavendish." If he was going to lie, then she would give him only what he asked and nothing more.

"A woman. Fascinating." He rubbed his chin which needed a shave and found a spot to scratch as he contemplated the woman who had made Rayne's hand. He was most likely deciding whether Jasmine was worthy of his collection. After all that was what dragons did with unique people.

"She is married to a dragon." Rayne stalled his plans with this free bit of information.

"Too late then," he jokingly commented. Obviously not heart broken by not being able to collect Jasmine.

Taking control of the conversation again she brought them back to the interrogation. "Do you know who murdered your wife?"

"Yes, Sebastian Karmel, otherwise known as Head Basher Karmel. Why do they call you Lady Golden Hand?"

He had clearly been asking about her as he hadn't known her nickname last night when they had first met. Who he had been talking to while in this state she wasn't sure but she didn't pry either. She suppressed the sigh. "When I was about ten, my father had my first hand made. It was rudimentary with a brass claw. Of course, others mocked me for it but they also wanted an easy cover if my father ever heard the name. Golden Hand can be complimentary but really it was to degrade me. I don't answer to the name."

His whiskey gold eyes sparked with amusement, which she didn't appreciate. He was worse than Everett who always thought the name was comical and apt. "You should take it back for your own."

Rayne flushed red but didn't take the bait. "Did you ever meet Sebastian?" She had seen the name in the records. So, the man had been pardoned but eventually had paid for the crime. That was if he was truly guilty. She wasn't entirely sure of that.

"Yes. He worked for Eleanor. When I found out they were going to pardon him I thought I would confront him. He was at the Maiden Hare. Drunk. He mocked me for being impotent. I left, I left Londinium altogether. How does it work?"

"I haven't the foggiest." She flexed the hand so he could see the extent of its abilities.

"That isn't fair, I answered your questions." He dramatically pouted, putting debutantes to shame with the fat lip. At least he dropped the subtly from his manipulations.

"You have kept things from me." They all looked towards the door as they heard knocking. Larkin went to see who would be knocking on the door of the dragon as it was clear the dragon wasn't in any condition to be welcoming anyone or expecting guests.

Alone with the dragon for the moment he leaned forward and said, "Have you ever considered being in a dragon's collection?"

Her brows shot together. "I'm not anyone's slave, dragon, so you can forget all that. If you are offering marriage though, I think you need to look at your own suitability."

She waved to indicate his unkempt state.

Larkin returned with a small runner. Rayne fished out a coin for the boy who worked for Scotland Yard. Larkin relayed the boy's message while she paid him.

"A head was found in the river. Since we're the only ones missing one, they think we might be interested."

Rayne turned to Victor as she got to her feet. "We'll be in contact."

"I'll come with you." He rose to his feet with more grace than she expected from his appearance.

"I don't think you're in much of a state to do anything, sir." He was probably capable but it was an easy excuse.

"I can take you there as a dragon." He flapped a hand to indicate he meant flying.

"No, you're unlikely to be able to carry two people and we don't want to scare the public." She knew some of the lore around dragons and flying. They were not pack animals and it meant something more significant to offer a human a ride. She narrowed her eyes as she took him in. He was trying to manipulate her again and he had gone back to being sneaky about it.

He snorted. "Nothing fazes the people of Londinium, let alone a dragon. I can carry both of you." She glanced at Larkin. It would be significantly faster but she knew her stalwart companion was not a fan of new experiences. She wanted to know what Victor was up to. Surely it couldn't simply be an urge to collect a woman with a golden hand. Besides, she knew he was keeping something from her and she needed to be around him long enough to find out what he was hiding.

Larkin shrugged. "It'd be a story to tell the boys." She shook her head at the lengths men would go to be able to hold one over the other. She turned back to Victor to study him. He was an open book emotionally. She would be able to tell if he was the killer the moment he saw the head. She might not know yet what he wanted from her but she could use it for her own benefit.

"Fine, you can take us but you're to follow my lead. I don't have loose cannons on my case."

Chapter Seven

The river was the catch-all of everything in the city. The water wasn't drinkable as all human waste eventually ended up in the water. Where the severed head went into the water was anyone's guess, that it ended up in the refuse barge was no surprise.

These enterprising men scavenged off the river interesting flotsam that found its way to the water. Their occupation had its disadvantages. One being they smelt as bad as the river. Thankfully, it was not summer. The river could make a person faint in the middle of the summer. One of the reasons her family escaped to the country when they could. Her job had taught her the true torture of the warmer seasons in the city.

The two tall men stood with the officer from the Yard. The men looked nervous while the officer chatted up a local woman, oblivious to the witnesses he was supposed to be watching. The scavengers, too scared to try to escape, left the officer to find his own amusement while they waited for them to arrive. She didn't approve of the officer's lax attitude towards his work but he was not alone in his lackadaisical work ethic.

Rayne sent the officer on his way and turned to the scavengers to ask, "Want to show me your prize?"

The taller of the men ignored her question and instead asked, "Is that a dragon?" He motioned with a short nod of his head towards Victor. Considering they had made a very dramatic entrance she had expected them to make some reference to the dragon.

Victor, who had managed to change after transporting them, flashed his teeth in an attempt at charm. "Why, yes, I am. Did you see me fly in? I'm fantastic, aren't I?" Humility was not Victor's failing.

"Are you going to eat us?" the other shorter man asked.

"No, you are way too odorous for that," Victor assured them.

The other man smacked the taller man in the arm. "I told you the dragon wasn't gonna be interested in the likes of us."

Rayne prompted, "The head?" They waved to the cart they had brought in from their boat. Rags, and other odds and ends; disguised the head. Rayne used a handkerchief with her real hand. There was no way she wanted to have anything from the river in the creases of her hand. There was a line she wouldn't cross. Twisting the head, she turned the bloated mass, so the features were visible. She kept her peripheral vision on Victor to see his reaction.

He looked pale and said in a soft voice, "It's him. Sebastian." She knew it would be. Londinium was large but they were not at a stage where heads floating in the Thames was an everyday occurrence. But why did Sebastian who was supposed to be Eleanor's killer have her wedding ring?

Larkin asked, "Did you kill him?" Larkin was a good partner even if he still insisted she be ladylike.

Victor shook his head. "I didn't kill him years ago when he first escaped, there is no reason for me to kill him now."

Rayne straightened, folding the handkerchief so none of the soiled part would touch her pocket when she returned it there. "He killed your wife. I thought dragons looked after their collections."

"It is more complicated than that." It must be that secret embarrassment he hadn't wanted to speak about when she was interrogating him.

"You can 'uncomplicate' it and tell us everything you know." She wasn't about to make it easy for him. She wasn't a fan of lies and she knew he was keeping something from her.

"I'll reveal all I know to others in my collection," he purred the words.

She knew what the offer meant. She would have to be his mistress before he would let her in to his confidence.

"Then I will have to ferret out your secrets in another way." Rayne wasn't going to allow him to manipulate her. Her mother was the only one who had that right.

———

Rayne looked at the case notes she had made. Twirling, the now clean, gold ring in her fingers as she contemplated what she already knew about this case. She could chase down the dragon's or Sebastian's secrets. At least Sebastian's were easier to obtain. Her boss wouldn't be very pleased she was still on the case. The death of a suspected murderer would be very low on Maynes' list. She already had another case on her desk to investigate.

Before Rayne could decide on a path to take in her investigation her mother swept into the office. "What an abysmal place, has no one heard of wallpaper?"

"Mother?" Rayne half rose from her seat.

"Yes, dear?" Lady Ancaster replied sarcastically as if she didn't know why Rayne was so astonished to see her in Rayne's workplace when her mother had never visited before.

"No, I mean, what are you doing here, mother? You never come into my work." Rayne returned to her seat, keeping her eyes on her. There must be a strategy her mother was employing here and that meant Lady Ancaster wanted something.

Lady Ancaster gazed around the room, studying the minimum of furniture with a wrinkle of her nose. "I should have before. There is a real need for a woman's touch on this place. I don't know how you can come here every day and not get the urge to decorate. At least put up a painting or tapestry to hide those horrific walls." Her eyes stopped on the articles from the cases she had solved which had managed to get into a newspaper. Most were penny dreadful quality as she didn't often deal with important cases.

"You haven't answered me," Rayne urged her to get to the favour she wanted as there was no other reason her mother would visit her at work.

Lady Ancaster snapped her fan closed and put it away in her reticule before she answered, "I came bearing good news. You have a marriage offer."

Rayne laid her face down in her hands. She mumbled into her hands, "Kill me now."

Before she had managed to convince her mother not to worry about her marriage prospects because they didn't exist. With an offer, even an unsuitable one, she would never be able to stop her mother from turning predatory in gaining her a mate.

Her mother, oblivious to her distress, continued, "A lovely gentleman. His name is Victor."

That last part had Rayne shooting up to her feet. "Don't tell me he talked to Papa."

"Yes, he did. A charming fellow." Lady Ancaster ignored Rayne's dramatic reaction to finding out the dragon had offered for her.

"He is a dragon," Rayne said, incredulous. She was aware her mother probably knew but Rayne wanted to make sure her mother understood she wasn't interested in marrying a dragon even if most of the ton thought they were the ideal match. Anyone married to a dragon were instantly rich, healthy as a horse and could live for centuries instead of decades. Rayne wasn't sure the cost was worth it.

"I know that. Why do you think we even entertained him? Only the best for our little flower." Her mother's cheeks were bright with her excitement.

"I am not a flower." Rayne gritted her teeth.

"To us you are. I take it you are familiar with Victor."

Rayne flopped back into her chair. She had to find a way to discourage her mother. "Yes, he is a suspect in my murder case."

"Oh dear, that will not do. We can't have a murderer in the family. The scandal would be terrible to bear...I know." She clapped her hands, excited by her plan. "You get to work and solve the case and prove that he isn't the killer. Then you can marry him." Clearly her mother didn't think Victor was the killer. Rayne had to agree but she couldn't let her feelings keep her from investigating.

"Mother, I thought we had come to an agreement on this. I'm not going to marry." Rayne was desperate by this stage.

"No, you decided you were unlikely to marry because of your little imperfection. We humoured you and allowed you to pursue your career. There is no harm in a woman having a purpose. That doesn't mean it precludes marriage and babies." The last was said with outright glee from her mother.

"Pester Everett for babies. He is old enough to marry." Rayne had no qualms of throwing her brother in front of their mother as cannon fodder.

"He's nineteen. Way too young. Besides, he is off to Oxford later in the year. He is going to educate himself." The emphasis on educate made Rayne sigh. Everett was smart. He didn't need any coddling from their mother but as the only boy he was destined to be wrapped in cotton wool at any opportunity. Though she doubted Everett would go to Oxford. Despite his good grades he hadn't made friends with any of his teachers or classmates with his liberal views.

Rayne's voice was just a little sharp as she stated to her mother, "Well, if you're going to play messenger then you can go back to Papa and tell him the dragon is not suitable."

Lady Ancaster wasn't immune to Rayne's tone and she frowned. "Let us not be hasty."

"Mother." Rayne wasn't going to back down from this.

"Fine, we'll make him go on his way but you know dragons. They are persistent."

Her mother left with a dramatic flourish of her skirt. Larkin said from the door, "I see where you get your skill with interrogating people. Your mother is persistent herself."

"Only because she loves us." Rayne quickly defended her mother. Though at that moment she could wish her mother loved her just a little less.

"You keep telling yourself that. What are our plans for the day?" Larkin wasn't about to let domestic dramas get between him and the case, an aspect of his personality that allowed him to work with her in the early days when no one else would.

"We're going to the Maiden's Hare. See why the place was so popular with Sebastian. Maybe they can tell us more about Sebastian."

CHAPTER EIGHT

The Maiden's Hare was busy for daylight hours. Not that Rayne thought any of the current clientele actually knew it was during the day. The windows were non-existent, a common thing in poor areas of town. The poor had found ingenious ways to avoid the tax but it put the poorer folk into uninhabitable situations. The inn was one of these. Her boots squelched on soaked floors as she made her way to the back of the public house where the owner cleaned chipped mugs with a rag. He grunted in greeting as they approached.

"Sir, do you know who Sebastian Karmel is? You might have known him as Head Basher."

He put away a mug as he answered, "I know him."

"Was he here recently?" People were still suspicious of bobbies but compared to previous years they begrudgingly cooperated with the police force.

"A couple of days ago but before that I have nah seen him in years. He just showed up out of nowhere along with that peeler."

"Peeler?" This was interesting.

"Yeah, he sat over there." He motioned with the rag in his hand to a table in the corner of the room.

"A peeler came in. Seen him in the newspapers, I have. Well, he sat down with Basher and they got into an argument. Basher left and the peeler stayed for a bit then left as well. That was the day they found the bits of person out back." He picked up another mug. This one in worse shape than the one he had just cleaned. It amazed Rayne that his customers didn't bleed to death every time they drank.

"Could the peeler have been his killer?" She mused more to herself than to the publican.

The owner snorted. "Hardly. Peelers don't go around killing people like Basher. Besides Basher was a pug, he wouldn't have let some measly peeler take him down, no matter the bobby knocker." Strange to see someone so naïve in this neighbourhood. Anyone could be taken by surprise, even the best fighter.

"Do you remember the name of the peeler?" Rayne asked more hopeful than anything else. The owner shrugged. The implication of a policeman involved had Rayne frowning as she thanked the owner. Larkin had been at her back but he watched the rest of the crowd. She wasn't sure if he had been listening or not.

She asked, "Did you hear?" Her tone speculative as she pondered on who the mysterious peeler was, to firstly be placed in the newspapers then appear here. There weren't many of them who had managed that notoriety or fame. She knew her godfather Sir Rowan Charles had graced a page or two of the newspaper but she was sure it wasn't him. He couldn't be the only peeler to be in the newspapers.

"Yeah, one of us has gone rogue." Larkin was more cavalier with the information, so she knew he hadn't thought it all the way through. It wasn't unheard of for officers to do the wrong thing but she doubted any of them had managed to get into the papers.

"There could be another explanation," she hoped wistfully.

"Doubtful. Not all of us are saints. You keep yourself safe when talking about this with the others." Maybe he did understand the implications. Which reminded her about Lady Beechworth and her blackmailer.

"Has there been a peeler that was fired before I came on board? Someone who was willing to break the rules?"

"There have been a few."

He was cautious with his words, so she added, "A peeler willing to blackmail people."

Larkin grunted. "That'd be Markim. Slippery bugger. He was barely on the job for a year before his true colours shone. Is he still up to his ways?"

"It seems like it. Will there be backlash if I bring him in?" She was still concerned about her standing with the other officers.

"Unlikely. They might grumble about looking after our own but he was a blackguard before he joined and he didn't change. They'd thank you if you put an end to his ways if they had the guts for it. But when you do, make sure you stick by me. Wouldn't want anyone to think they are upholding his honour or nothing."

"You break my heart, Larkin, I never knew you felt that way." Larkin frowned in confusion and then his face darkened when he realised she was teasing him. He didn't like it when she teased him but sometimes it was too easy. She motioned for them to leave the pub. "Come, I have some other leads for us to follow. We'll leave Markim, the blackmailer, for another day. At the moment we have to hunt down Basher's story."

"I know Basher," The man leaning back on a chair by the door announced. "I knew his girl to." Larkin made an aborted protest and it was more squeak than grunt as she took a seat at the man's table. Unlike the owner who would help because he wanted the crime to be lower around his business this man wouldn't be so altruistic.

"Tell me." She put a coin on the table.

The man's eyes followed the coin as he spoke, "Basher was a clever fella, had a good setup. His girl would do all the work and he would protect her back when the mark got mad. They'd sell off everything together and go to a small village on the coast to lie low for a while. Basher's Pop had a cottage out there."

Another coin joined the other. "You know about the girl?" she encouraged.

"Eleanor? She was a looker. Knew how to sway her hips but wasn't the kind to flip her skirts casually. A classy girl that one. Pity that she died. That bastard dragon didn't need to kill her."

The revelation of the Eleanor as a con artist was hard to keep off her face. This was the secret Victor had been keeping from her. Instead of clearing him it only gave him motivation to have killed her. "You mean the dragon killed her?"

"Well, yeah. Basher loved that girl. He wouldn't have knocked her off, no matter what they said." So why did Victor and the courts think Sebastian had killed Eleanor? The notes she had found in the archive backed him up as Sebastian was convicted even if he was later pardoned. What if the outcome of the trial was wrong? That could explain why he had been pardoned by the Governor if he had known something others didn't.

Another coin was added and she asked, "You know the name of that village?"

"Something that starts with Haven. Haven Blue or Haven Sand. I can't remember."

Rayne beamed a charming smile. "Thank you." That was all the man knew.

"I have stories about the other crooked people here." He rubbed one of the coins thoughtfully.

"I'm sure you do, but I only needed to know about Basher. I'll come to you for my next case. You might have something to tell me then."

His disappointment was short lived as he rolled the coins in his hand. "Sure, Lady Golden Hand." Unlike the ton there was no derision in his tone. Maybe her brother and the dragon were right. Maybe she could take the name back.

When Rayne dragged herself home, she was surprised by the small family gathering. Her family all had their own lives, so they rarely gathered together like this. She joined them and flopped into the couch next to her sister, Katherine.

Rayne asked, "This isn't some ambush to get me to marry the dragon?" She sat up and eyed them all suspiciously when they didn't instantly say she was being ridiculous. When they looked confused, she accepted that wasn't the point of the gathering and returned to a more casual pose on the chair.

"The dragon offered for you? Should we be forcing you to marry him?" This came from Everett. He was the only one shocked by the news. Her sister had known about it. A little surprising since Katherine hardly ever raised her head for rumours, even family rumours.

Her mother said, "No, if anything we want you all to marry who you wish. The last thing we would like for you all is to be trapped in a marriage. That is a lifetime of torture. We think you need to have a good person by your side."

"So, if you aren't all here to pressure me into marrying the dragon then what is this family gathering about?" Rayne waved her hand to indicate the family. Everyone except their sister, who was on the continent.

Her father said, "We got a letter from your sister and were reading it."

"How is she doing?" There was only four years between her and her oldest sister, and their interests were so different that they had never really been able to see eye to eye. That didn't preclude her love for her sister. A condition that wouldn't change despite distance or interests.

"Bored," Her father announced. "She is finally figuring out that chasing an arrangement with a dragon isn't what she wants."

"What does she want?" Rayne thought someone amongst the horde would understand their sister even if Rayne didn't.

Her mother answered with a slight snort, "Children, of course. She wants to have little ones. Everything else in her life is icing. She'll figure it out." Rayne was glad her parents understood their children and allowed them to follow what they needed. There was no way Rayne would be where she was now without them.

That had her asking, "What would you do if I got fired from my job?"

So far, she was planning to arrest an ex-bobby and it was becoming evident that another prominent officer was involved in another crime. If it wasn't an officer, it was the dragon and she knew she would be the sacrificial lamb to the god of political expedience if she had to arrest Victor.

Her father asked, "Charles wouldn't allow that, would he?"

"He might. You see, I'm pretty sure there is someone in the department who is a killer. There are too many questions and not enough answers but I'm scared that at the end of this thread I'm pulling it will reveal a dirty peeler." She didn't tell them about the blackmailer as she didn't want them to ask any questions she couldn't answer.

Her brother realised the issue straight away as he said, "No one wants egg on their face. They might sacrifice you to get rid of the embarrassment." No one said they would be happy to get rid of her because of her gender and that this would merely be the excuse.

Her father hummed thoughtfully and her mother said, "It shouldn't matter. The whole reason you're there is to help people. You can't let a murderer go."

"What if it embarrassed Uncle Charles?" Rayne pressed.

"He wouldn't care. It would be others that would put the pressure on you," Lady Ancaster stated with some authority. Since her and Charles had been friends since childhood, she might have a reason for her confidence. Maybe Lady Beechworth was right and she really was bulletproof when it came to her job.

Her sister said, "Whether you finish this or not there will always be a murderer in the department. If you don't find them, someone else will. Though probably after someone else dies."

Her father nodded. "We'll support you; you know that. Go with your heart."

"You all know that I'm going to go after the murderer," Rayne answered the question in her father's voice.

Everett snorted. "That is a given."

Rayne shook her head at the ridiculousness of a ducal family encouraging her to scandalise their name. "You know if it isn't a peeler then it is the dragon."

"The one that wants to marry you?" Katherine asked over her book.

Everett poked Rayne in the side and she snarled at him, "He wants to marry my hand not me."

Her father said, "He is unlikely to kill you." As if that had ever been one of her concerns, she thought sarcastically to herself. Though she had to admit her father had a point. Marriage was a risky business amongst most classes. She knew better than anyone in the family that most murders of women were committed by their husbands or lover. Her father though didn't dispel the idea that the dragon was only interested in her because of her brass hand. Dragons were not to be taken lightly though. For centuries they had been the only predator of human beings.

To assume, because of the treaty, Victor wasn't violent was naïve. "He could have killed his wife," Rayne said though she didn't even sound convincing to herself.

"You don't believe that," her mother stated. Again, that authority still in her voice. This time because she knew Rayne.

Rayne felt perverse, so she asked, "Yeah and why not?"

"Because you like him." Her mother flashed her a smile. Sure her manipulation would eventually see fruit.

"Only you would think that, mom." There would be endless conversations about Victor as a suitor. His possibility of being a murderer wasn't a deal breaker for Lady Ancaster, apparently.

Her mother nodded her head with finality. "You do."

Rayne groaned and put an arm over her eyes. "I thought there wouldn't be any pressure to marry the dragon."

"No pressure just an insight." Her mother defended her pressure to marry the dragon.

Rayne shook her head at the ridiculousness of it all. She got to her feet and said, "I'm going to bed. Don't do anything stupid." Though she was hoping for a miracle.

CHAPTER NINE

"Why are we back here?" Larkin asked this as they were again outside the residence of the dragon. He already knew she didn't suspect him of the murder. Though others in the office were all convinced he had killed Sebastian and Eleanor.

Rayne tugged on her coat to straighten it. Not afraid that Larkin would comment on it anymore. "You heard the man at the pub. All he knew was that the man meeting Sebastian was a famous policeman. We can't take what we know back there. We don't know who we can trust. But the dragon was there during the investigation. Also, I want to know if he killed Eleanor." She was pretty sure he hadn't killed Sebastian as he was right. If he was going to kill the man, it would have been years ago. And she was sure they wouldn't have found any part of his body at all. Eleanor's demise had too many questions that she hoped the dragon could answer.

Larkin frowned. "Are you sure you want to confront him if you think he is the killer?"

"Yes." Mostly because she didn't think he was the killer but she had to follow the lead. A dragon wouldn't need to dump a body in the river. Eleanor could have disappeared and Victor could have admitted that she was a thief and that she had run away. No one would have questioned him whether he had merely eaten her. The dumping in the river was what a human would do. A falling out amongst thieves was more likely or someone had noticed Eleanor in the wrong neighbourhood with a lot of wealth and had thought to relieve her of it.

This theory didn't explain how Sebastian got Eleanor's ring or why he kept it if it was a falling out amongst thieves. There just were too many questions and at the moment the dragon was her only source of information.

This time when the dragon opened the door he was dressed for guests. His face lit up and he reached for her hands. Rayne stumbled back, out of his reach.

Victor frowned at her recoil. "You haven't come to accept my proposal?"

"What? No." She had forgotten he had gone to her father to ask for her hand. His face dropped. Shaking himself he recovered a little. Enough that he stepped aside so they could enter and led the way into the sitting room. It had since been cleaned and the colour had returned to much of the once dust coated furniture. Everything gleamed with a tender touch and brass and silver reflected the light. If he hadn't hired servants since she had first spoken to him then he had certainly done a decent job of cleaning himself. He sat on the love seat and patted it to encourage her to sit down.

Rayne instead went for shock factor. "Your wife was a con artist."

He glanced at the seat and gave up trying to get her to sit with him. "Thief as well," he admitted while he eyed Larkin. "This is not something I feel comfortable speaking about amongst strangers."

"Larkin is hardly a stranger." Though she wasn't sure why she was exempt from the stranger status. She had only spoken with Victor a handful of times and always with an audience. Did he believe his offer for her hand gave them a connection that didn't exist?

Victor gave her an inscrutable look so she added, "Fine. Larkin you can go. I'll be heading home after this."

"Are you sure, my lady? He's a dragon." What he meant was he was a suspect for murder. That might be where the clues were leading but Rayne had a hunch there was more to it all and she was willing to risk her life on it. Obviously, she hadn't convinced him yet of the dragon's innocence or was he more convinced that it couldn't be a fellow peeler.

"I'm sure he will abide by the treaty," Rayne reassured him. Larkin grunted but tipped his hat in farewell and left. Victor patted the couch next to him. She shook her head. There was no reason to tempt the dragon with proximity.

He didn't seem disappointed. Instead, he hopped up and said, "Come look at my collection." He didn't wait for her agreement and led her out of the room. Forced to follow or be left alone in the parlour she followed him as he made his way to a long gallery. She had expected art instead there were pedestals with glass cabinets framed in a deep mahogany. Inside were specimens she never expected in a dragon's home. The first one was a broken cog.

Victor beamed and said, "This is from the textile factory I collected when I first came to England. It took longer than expected to collect the gold I needed to get what I wanted. The owner was a brute and beat his workers till they were unable to work then he would fire them and hire children for half the price. One even died." The cog was the cleanest cog she had ever seen. It glistened. It had certainly seen more care than the house had when she had first come to question him. She wasn't sure whether the neatness was a new thing along with clean-up of the rest of the house.

Victor glowed with pride. "It won the most productive mill last year. Even though they have two days off a week and only work forty hours. I hope others will follow the trend."

Rayne followed him as he went to the next cabinet.

She stalled him before he explained the next item, "Tell me about Eleanor."

The light of pride dimmed considerably as he stopped by the new cabinet. Inside was a single embroidered handkerchief. He tapped the edge of the framed glass as he thought. He had probably thought he would never have to articulate this story to anyone, so she allowed him time to find his words.

"I met her at an inn just outside the city. Not that it mattered where I met her. It was a reputable place and her carriage had broken down and she was forced to walk. Her footman carried her things. That was Sebastian. I didn't know it was a show. She was charming and intelligent. We spent the night debating the merits of different laws in the Empire compared to the other countries. She rode with me the next day. I bonded with her that night. Within a week she had figured how to steal everything that wasn't bolted down. She left one day while I was out. I put out that she was kidnapped as I didn't want to reveal her betrayal."

She winced. "That is honest."

"Dragons usually are honest. We tend to lose our powers if we start to lie." That was a bit of dragon lore she wasn't familiar with. She would have to ask her father the validity of his claim. In the meantime, she would take everything he said with the pinch of salt required of every detective.

"But you didn't find her. She was found floating in the Thames a few days later. What happened when the police became involved?"

"This was before the police. It was one of the cases that convinced the local government to instigate a policing system like the continent has. They found out she had a lover. He was passed out, drunk in the Maiden's Hare with her blood under his fingernails. He confessed after that. But that wasn't enough."

Rayne frowned confused. "Why did they pardon him then?" She had assumed there was some circumstantial evidence that had been ambiguous enough to convince the Governor.

"Politics. The Governor didn't like dragons. He thought we were invaders. He didn't last long but he lasted long enough to bury the evidence and give Sebastian a pardon. When my lawyer told me there was no way to get a conviction when the Governor himself was against me, I confronted Sebastian. I left the city after that. Since you found his body chopped up only the other day, you must know I left him alive. I have no motive to wait all this time to find him now."

She believed him for now as it mirrored her own thoughts on the murder. "Do you know what happened to him when you left town?"

"No. I was frustrated with the system. Eleanor and Sebastian were merely a symptom of what is wrong here, so I went away."

He stepped away from the glass cabinets. "You don't think I killed her or Sebastian."

It wasn't a question but she answered it anyway, "No. I think you would have saved yourself the hassle of this investigation and just eaten them. I think this was done by a human."

He flashed her a grin. "It wasn't my charm that convinced you of my innocence. So, when you close this case will you accept my proposal?"

Would she never be able to convince those around her she wasn't interested in a relationship that would turn her into a virtual slave? "No. I turned you down because I'm never going to marry."

His voice was thoughtful as his eyes dropped from her own, "So it isn't a dragon thing?"

Rayne wanted him to know all the reasons she wouldn't accept his proposal, so he didn't get his hopes up that she might change her mind one day. "Yes, that as well. You guys keep slaves."

He growled in frustration. "It isn't slavery."

She wasn't convinced by his fierce denial. "You can call it whatever you like, it is slavery."

"It is a reciprocal slavery. You would own me." As if that would make the prospect any more palatable.

"That still isn't very appealing. You haven't been able to show your best side." So far, she had seen his temper and his entanglement in a confidence scam. Not flattering in the least.

"No. I suppose not. Normally I show off my chemistry skills. But can I tempt you?" His voice was so hopeful she felt sympathy for him but she wasn't sure what was talking about until he laid his hand on her waist. She knew she should step back, that if she gave him any indication, he would always chase her. But she was tempted as well.

He was striking and interesting, and what other time would she have a chance to kiss a dragon. He placed his other hand gently on her cheek. The warmth seeped into her. His proximity warmed her deeper than the touch. Turning her insides into a quivery jelly.

Victor's gaze was on her lips. "Step away now if you don't want me to." Her answer was to lick her lips.

He lowered his head slowly. His lips grazed hers. Asking permission. She opened her lips and merged with Victor. She stepped towards him. All her senses drawn to where they were pressed together. She brought her own hand up and laid it on his shoulder. The lack of heightened sensory connection brought her back to reality.

She touched him with her mechanical hand. The hand that was the only reason the dragon even desired her as dragons only collected unique things.

Rayne stumbled away. Catching herself on the pedestal behind her. Victor didn't follow her.

He stood with his arms limp beside him as he asked wistfully, "Rayne?"

"We are not that familiar, sir." Her voice harsher than she intended. It was because she felt as a fool to even give in to the temptation he had offered. She couldn't even pretend he had manipulated her into the situation as he had made his desires very clear.

"I think we are but I will call you Miss Ancaster if that is your wish." His voice sad though he had reverted to her more formal title at least.

"It is and we can't do this again." She straightened and tugged on her coat to neaten the line. It also gave her something to do, her eyes steadfastly lowered.

He asked, "This?"

She waved a hand to indicate the two of them. "*This.*"

A smile only touched the corner of his mouth. "You mean the kiss?"

Heat stained her cheeks and she ran a finger around the starched collar of her coat. Angry that he teased her instead of having a serious conversation. "Yes, because I am not going to be in your collection." To remind herself just as much to remind him why she would never be able to take their desires any further.

"I know. You told me. But is an affair off the table?" His wistful tone made her steam. He only wished to collect her as a trophy. It wasn't her he wanted.

"Yes." She growled.

His face dropped. She had been propositioned before but this was certainly the most unique. Rayne muttered some excuses and made her escape. Everything Victor was confused her. He was arrogant and possessive. But he was also clever and handsome. It didn't help that her own feelings were only more confusing.

CHAPTER TEN

Rayne had barely stepped into her house when her fourteen-year-old sister, Katherine, barrelled into her. "Perfect. You can take me shopping."

Katherine caught her hand and dragged her outside to the carriage that had just delivered Rayne. "Macy is ill and I desperately need to get out of the house." Katherine turned to the driver and gave instructions. The carriage was already moving before Rayne could even come up with a few excuses for why she shouldn't go shopping with her sister.

Instead of whining Rayne asked, "What are we shopping for?"

"Books." Of course, Rayne wasn't even sure why she asked. Her sister was on an endless quest for more knowledge.

"Surely you have enough. Father even gave you a wall in the library for the books, so you have a place to store them."

"I'm starting a new field of study." Of all the duke's children Katherine was the most brilliant. She preferred science and every year she got excited about a new experiment or field. She had outstripped every school and tutor their father could find for her.

Rayne asked, knowing the answer would be amusing, "What are you studying now?"

"Electricity. I thought I'd see if I could bring something back to life."

Last month Rayne had arrested a man for stealing bodies from the cemetery. She remembered telling Katherine about it. She hoped that hadn't sparked her interest in this new study. Her parents wouldn't appreciate another daughter playing with the dead.

"Life? And just what are you going to bring back to life."

Katherine waved off her concerns airily. "Animals at first, then I think I'll see if I can reanimate people."

"You know there is an illegal trade in bodies?" Rayne assumed Katherine remembered the conversation last month so didn't add any more details.

"Yes, they wouldn't be able to help me. I've decided that anything I bring back needs to be recently deceased. Body traders would have to kill someone to bring me something fresh enough. No, I'm planning to go to a hospital and talk with people who are dying. Get their permission first. It only seems right if you are going to be mucking around with their bits." Some foresight on her sister's part and certainly more ethical than other comments from her sister. It seemed the pursuit of science was enough to wipe out many sane objections. Though she didn't want to ask what her fourteen-year-old sister meant by bits. This plan at least would avoid Rayne having to arrest Katherine when she got into trouble with body traders.

"You couldn't be a normal sister and want to go buy ribbons," Rayne lamented.

"You are thinking of Amelia." Amelia was the oldest of all the siblings and was in Europe. She was the epitome of a lady. She had gone to Europe to find a dragon husband. She had heard the stories like the rest of them at father's knee and it was her dream to make a dragon match. Rayne wondered if she would get her dream or find a new one like Lady Ancaster thought and have children.

"She should have stayed. There is a dragon ready to marry right here," Rayne speculated out loud.

"You mean Victor? He seemed like a good sort. You should marry him."

Rayne knew they had spoken of the dragon the other night and Katherine certainly hadn't been surprised by the revelation that a dragon had come a courting. But Rayne hadn't realised that Katherine had met Victor.

"When did you meet him?" she demanded.

"When he came to speak to daddy. So why aren't you going to marry him?" So much for avoiding pressure from the family.

"I'm not going to be a slave," Rayne answered honestly hoping to pre-empt any other attempt to pressure her into a match with the dragon.

"It isn't really. Slavery, I mean." Katherine like their father had studied dragons and knew about their culture and their lore. But Rayne wasn't going to be fooled. Owning someone wasn't done amongst sentient beings. Ironically, the Wyvern Empire was the first country in the world to ban slavery. In the new world there was still slavery.

"What do you call collecting?" Rayne challenged.

"Actually, what they are doing is binding themselves at a molecular level in order to transfer matter to this plane. Apparently, they are out of sync enough that they can only be fertile if they have more of a link. They can only make things pop in and out when they have that bond. They call it collecting but really it is more a scientific phenomenon where our essence is entangled with theirs. Magical almost, if I actually believed in magic." Katherine probably knew more but kindly didn't bore her by going into any details.

Rayne tilted her head and asked, "Are you really fourteen?"

Katherine flashed a grin at the teasing. "The last time I counted, I was. Though I think at my next birthday, I'll try being sixty."

They hopped out at the bookstore. The patrons eyed them suspiciously as it was not common for a woman to be browsing scientific texts. Katherine though was oblivious and skipped through the shelves muttering to herself the author's name as she searched the shelves. Rayne checked out the section on forensics but there were no new texts so she went to stand outside so her sister wouldn't see her waiting and rush through her own shopping.

Rayne was debating whether to purchase some ices when Lady Beechworth sauntered down the street. "Afternoon Miss Ancaster. Any luck with my blackmailer?" At least Lady Beechworth was transparent and to the point. There was always the issue of the nobility feeling they could take advantage of their connections with the police. They'd usually sidled up ask and for a small, tiny favour. Of course, saying no made her look like a complete jerk so at least this was refreshing.

"No, I have a case. A murder actually." Lady Beechworth would also appreciate honesty in return.

"Oh, very gruesome. Someone we know?" Her voice a little more eager than was appropriate for a lady of the ton.

Rayne didn't see any reason not to tease her with some information. It would soon be in the papers. Keeping secrets from the press was impossible. The officers at the Yard didn't know the meaning of discretion. "The man who killed Victor's bride, Eleanor."

The spark of interest was clear in Lady Beechworth's eyes. "Anything juicy to tell me. I swear I won't spread it about."

"Of course, you will." Rayne chuckled as she responded to Lady Beechworth's ridiculous statement.

The smile grew on Lady Beechworth's lips. "Of course, I will. Well, dish."

"Nothing to dish." Rayne wasn't about to tell any of the gossiping ladies of the ton about Eleanor being a high-class thief who had conned a dragon into marrying her. She didn't think Victor would appreciate his shame being aired amongst the very judgemental high society.

To deflect Lady Beechworth she said, "I'll visit your blackmailer in the morning."

"Brilliant. It will ease my mind to have that all sorted." She patted Rayne's hand and sauntered off again. Rayne wondered if Lady Beechworth learned her manipulation skills from Rayne's mother or if it was merely a generational skill.

Katherine said from the store doorway, "She didn't eat you alive. What is your secret?"

"There isn't anything wrong with Lady Beechworth. She is one of the few who still goes out of her way to talk with me."

Katherine shuddered dramatically. "She scares the bejeebus out of me."

"Just talk about your science stuff. She will appreciate that you have a mind."

Katherine eyed Rayne suspiciously. "What did she want to talk to you about? Your investigations?"

"In a manner. Come, let's go for an ice." There was no way she would talk to her sister about the blackmailer. Rayne understood the need for silence due to someone's reputation. But she was also aware that her sister was only fourteen and didn't need to know all the gruesome details of her work. Besides Rayne had a healthy respect for someone's reputation. Everyone had assumed hers was non-existence because of her physical damage. She knew better than anyone it was impossible to recover a reputation once it was gone.

CHAPTER ELEVEN

To give another level of discretion to Lady Beechworth's problem; Rayne went before work to the blackmailer's, Markim, address. He had done well as he lived in a decent part of town. With a park on the corner, the house was nestled in a quaint neighbourhood.

There was no evidence from the impatiens growing in the window that a villainous blackmailer lived there but Rayne trusted Lady Beechworth wasn't sending her on a wild goose chase. That the address Lady Beechworth had given her matched the one for Markim had been the deciding factor for Rayne about the validity of the blackmailing claims.

Rayne knocked on the door. It swung open with a soft whine. She poked her head into the house. There was a sense to the place that it was empty. A complete stillness that only an abandoned dwelling could have.

Even then Rayne hesitated on the threshold. "Anyone here?" No reply had Rayne entering.

She searched the rooms for signs of life. The house had sturdy furniture and though it was clear blackmailing was able to pay the bills, the owner of the house wasn't a collector of possessions. The front room was a male sanctuary with a set of leather seats. Cigar smoke permeated the wood. There wouldn't be any lady's tea served in that room.

She found the blackmailer's body in the parlour. There had been a struggle as chairs had been tipped over and the blackmailer's knuckles were bloody from fighting back.

The killer had used a convenient poker from the fireplace to cave in the side of the blackmailer's head and then had discarded the poker in a hurry. Rayne crouched down by the body. There was a pool of blood by his head. She peeled off her glove and pressed her hand to his neck. The skin was a little warmer than the room. This man had been dead a while but not days.

She picked up a wrist and dropped the hand. Rigor mortis had not set in so the deadly blow hadn't been too long ago. Her guess would be early hours of the morning or this side of midnight at the very latest.

Rayne turned away from his body and searched the room. Her first assumption was that an enemy of Markim had confronted him. Possibly one of his blackmail victims. There was no evidence of a search. Just of the fight. So, the killer either had the incriminating evidence or had panicked and left without it.

Rayne searched the drawers and shelves. She was looking for hidden compartments in the mantel when she saw something in the fireplace.

The grate was clean, ready for a fire to be laid. On the grate was ash and the single curl of a blackened piece of paper. Rayne tugged out a handkerchief with her metal hand and laid it out on her knee. She reached with her other hand and delicately placed the burned paper on the handkerchief. She couldn't make out the words on the blackened paper but she had heard dragons had abilities others didn't. She would see if Victor could help.

She found a small glass that she covered the paper with and wrapped the lot with the handkerchief. Keeping it all safe in her mechanical hand which she locked into position so nothing could jostle free. Travelling across town with her mechanical hand clamped shut was difficult as she kept forgetting and reached for things with her prosthetic hand only to pull herself up short so she didn't disturb the evidence.

Victor answered the door as usual when she knocked. He didn't make assumptions this time and frowned at her on his doorstep. "Miss Ancaster?" He had gone back to calling her by her more formal name. At least he kept to his word and her wishes.

"Are you able to read something off a piece paper that has been burned?"

He frowned at her in confusion but answered, "Yes."

She pushed past him into his house.

He asked, "Is this to do with Sebastian?"

"Not everything has to do with you, dragon. This is a new case."

"A murder?" It wasn't supposed to be. It was supposed to be a simple case of blackmail. At least now she didn't have to worry about aggravating some of the others at work by arresting Markim for blackmail. She might even get some credit from the peelers if she managed to solve his murder.

"Yes. So instead of interrogating me can you help me with this?" She offered the glass clamped in her mechanical hand.

"Of course." He led her through the house to a lab.

Rayne whistled when she saw it. "Is this something all dragons have in their homes?" There were tables covered in different machines. Glass tubes in trays and jars of mystery liquids bubbled away. He must have been working in here for things to still be on the go.

"No. We have our own specialities. I like chemicals. They are simple compared to the other sciences dragons enjoy."

"Simple?" She couldn't fathom a species that considered chemicals a hobby craft.

Rayne waved her hand at the equipment in the lab. "Can we proceed?" She offered him the handkerchief with the glass inside. The paper had shed some carbon, turning the handkerchief grey. Using some tweezers he pinched the paper with the care of a surgeon and placed it on a glass sheet. He then placed the glass over a tripod stand.

Victor spoke as he worked, "I didn't expect to see you back here after the way you left."

He meant the kiss and she was pleased he didn't actually say kiss as her cheeks were heating up just thinking of it. She answered honestly, "I don't know any other dragons."

Victor found that amusing rather than being offended. "We aren't all into science. Some of us can be downright moronic. You could have risked going to a dragon who wouldn't have been able to help you at all."

"Then consider this a compliment then, as I assumed you would be able to help." She watched him as he worked. His hand sure of his craft as he moved.

He flashed her a smile. "I will. Though I'd rather have you compliment my kissing abilities." So much for him not mentioning the kiss directly. Her cheeks bloomed like a summer rose with heat.

Rayne steeled some determination into her voice as she stated, "You can stop fishing for compliments as that isn't going to happen in this lifetime." She hoped he believed her as she didn't even believe herself and if he pushed, she just might give in.

"Is that a challenge?" She glared at him and he chuckled as he went back to his work.

He set a gas flame under the glass and said, "Come close as this will be quick." He turned up the flame, so it touched the glass. The words flared to life above the heat.

The note read, "Meet at the Maiden's Hare." The rest was unreadable.

She swore softly under her breath and Victor tutted mockingly, "Not very ladylike."

"Hunting killers isn't ladylike." Rayne had heard that tune from too many people that her answer was automatic. Her brain was going over the coincidence of two murders connected to the Maiden's Hare.

He couldn't be offended by the sharpness of her tone as he answered philosophically, "You should care about what you say as what we say had to first come from our minds."

Rayne took out a notebook and wrote down what had been visible on the note. "Don't lecture me, dragon. I have to find out who this blackmailer was blackmailing as that is who killed Sebastian." Snapping her notebook shut she spun on her heels and said over her shoulder, "Thank you, Victor."

"A pleasure." His voice a sensuous purr.

Chapter Twelve

L arkin laid a package on the desk. Rayne frowned, "What is this?"

"Rosie says every woman needs decent handkerchiefs. I did try to tell her you were a duke's daughter and had plenty." Rayne unwrapped the package. The handkerchiefs had her initials embroidered in the corner. Elegant, they were better than the set ordered by her mother from their own seamstress. Rosie had true talent.

"Tell her thank you. You can tell her I'll keep an eye on you to make sure you make it home every night." He snorted. As the muscle in their duo it was him who usually made sure Rayne came home. She put away the handkerchiefs. It was a thoughtful gesture.

Rayne went back to her notes. They were frustrating her. Rayne tapped a pencil on a pile of papers. She was supposed to be putting her notes on the case down on those pages but she was stuck with everything going through her head. Things pointed at the dragon except that he was too smart to leave too many clues leading to him. He was the only person who would want Sebastian dead.

Instead, it was someone who was pointing the evidence towards the dragon on purpose. A smart killer. Which was at odds at the brutal way that Sebastian was killed. The panicked murder and lack of planning in Markim's murder again didn't speak for any intelligence. Passion was more likely the motive in this violent act. Victor might feel honour bound to kill the person who had killed his wife but there was more feeling towards her betrayal than to the person who had killed her.

The mug of tea plonked onto her desk brought her out of her thoughts. Larkin flopped down in his chair and put his own mug up to his lips before he breathed over the hot liquid, "You are in a loop."

It wasn't a question but she answered, anyway. "Yes. I can't get my head around it all."

"Well, talk it out with me. Tell me what you think happened?" Larkin leaned back ready to listen to all the convoluted thoughts in her head.

They sometimes did this with difficult cases. As a sounding board he was trustworthy and always asked questions that untangled her thoughts like a greased chain. "If I had to do that, I'd have to go back to the first crime."

"The murder of Eleanor?" He took a contemplative sip of his tea. Larkin might be the muscle in their partnership but he was also a very good detective.

"No, the confidence fraud. They went after the dragon. That takes some guts. I don't think they came up with it themselves. I went to the Maiden's Hare today and spoke to some of Sebastian's old friends. Eleanor and Sebastian weren't known for taking on big fish. They were small-time crooks. They usually pulled their con on businessmen and low-ranking noblemen. Sebastian would work for them and find out what they were like and then Eleanor would arrive as their dream girl. She would sweep them off their feet and she would drain them of as much as possible. They were cautious and always finished the game long before the business men even knew they were being conned."

Rayne had to admire their skill. They had never over reached. Rayne picked up the cup. Larkin was a single man without a housekeeper so he knew how to make a decent cup of tea. He usually went a little sweeter than she liked. Sugar at least was more pleasant than honey in the subtle cup of tea.

"So, you think someone pointed them towards the dragon?" He asked.

"Yes. Sebastian didn't work for Victor. The dragon always takes servants in as part of their collection. He would have made sure Sebastian was worth collecting before making him a servant but when the dragon told me about meeting Eleanor, he said Sebastian was her servant not his. If Victor didn't know Sebastian then where did Eleanor get her information in order to play the role Victor wanted? Someone had to have told the two the information they needed to work the scam."

"So, a player we haven't met yet." He smiled, amused by the way she thought or by the idea of someone setting up the conmen.

"Or uncovered. The dragon had an enemy four years ago who is still around now. They are the one who is tying up loose ends." Rayne picked up the pencil and wrote down a question mark above Eleanor and Sebastian's names. She wrote down Victor's name as well with lines between all of them towards him. She then drew an x through the line to Eleanor.

"I don't think Sebastian killed her. I don't think Victor did either. Sebastian was used to this game and he couldn't play it without Eleanor. It would have been against his own well-being to kill her. It doesn't seem like he found another to play her part either. Instead, he ran off with his tail between his legs. But he also left with enough money to live well in the last four years. He was still wearing good clothes and he could afford to travel easily."

"Okay let's skip ahead to Sebastian's death then. Do you think he was killed by the other player?"

"I think it was that peeler." She hated the idea that one of her fellow co-workers was capable of murder and deceit. But not only that but a famous co-worker, as that would be the only way to be recognised from the papers and out of uniform.

"The one that met with Sebastian at the Hare?"

She took another sip as she thought. Taking her time, she added, "Sebastian was a conman. He escaped justice for that multiple times. Then there is the chance he killed Eleanor and again he escaped justice. Maybe it is a peeler who just wants justice." So, another player altogether or the same one who had set up the confidence scam?

It was a theory that could hold water but still it didn't sit right with her. Without knowing who the police officer was they would not be able to figure out the motive behind the murder or the targeting of Victor for the scam.

There was a perfunctory knock on the door and the boy who took around internal mail dropped something on the table. Rayne opened the note. It was a new case. A burglary on one of the more affluent streets. The people thought because she was from society that people would talk to her.

Unfortunately, society never spoke to peelers regardless of their parentage. Gathering her baton and tugging on her coat she flicked her head to indicate they had to leave.

———

Rayne rubbed her ear but the ringing wouldn't stop. She had forgotten how high pitched a hysterical woman could be. Even when they discovered the jewellery was borrowed rather than stolen, the pitch had gone to new octaves.

Larkin asked, "What?"

She flashed a smile. He must be hearing a ringing in his own ears. Before she answered her eyes caught on a sign hanging above the door ahead of them. It was for the Times. One of her father's favourite newspapers, as there was a journalist there that managed to get stories weeks before others.

Instead of admitting that she hadn't said anything at all she pointed to the newspaper and said, "I just need to stop in there."

Aware of her penchant for collecting papers for her father he asked, "Haven't you done your paper shopping for the week?"

"I want to see something. It won't take long and we didn't spend so much time on this case as we would've." They'd spent less than an hour dealing with the squealing mistress who had her jewellery borrowed by her teenage daughter.

Larkin gave in with a grunt and veered towards the entrance to the newspaper.

They were assaulted with noise as they entered the room. Large metal machines hissed and clunked as they rolled sheets of rag paper. The machine dominated the room.

Recoiling back when a man popped up from behind the press, Rayne covered her surprise quickly. He motioned for them to follow him. They made their way around the machine and the heat of the boiler.

Once in the other room Larkin closed the door. It didn't get rid of all the sound it made it bearable. After the screeching of the mistress and the machine she missed the man's first words.

Rayne shook her head to gather herself and said, "Sorry. I'm Rayne and this is Larkin. We were hoping you stored your plates."

The man offered a hand. "Thomas Barnes. I'm the editor here." It also appeared he was everything at the newspaper as they were as yet to see anyone else at the press.

He jerked a thumb over his shoulder. "We never throw anything away. A plate is expensive to make. Any idea what you're looking for?"

She shifted sideways as she made her way past moving machinery and followed the newspaper man farther into the building. "We're looking for images of peelers."

Thomas hummed speculatively. "That will be a few years ago. I find you fellas boring so I avoid stories to do with you."

"Is that a compliment or an insult?" Rayne asked with a bit of a smile. Thomas blinked as if he hadn't realised he had insulted them.

He recovered and flashed a grin. "Take it as a compliment. I only like to chase scandals."

He ran a hand through hair that was in need of a cut. He must have remembered why they were there as he jerked into motion. "We keep the plates back here. Sometimes we can reuse the more generic ones. Thought about putting out some of those penny sheets but we struggle to keep up with the demand for the paper."

"Yours is my father's favourite." Rayne collected papers for her father who used them to analyse what was happening around the world. He could speculate on the smallest amount of information and be accurate enough that the government often used his services to make large trade deals and decisions. Thomas skipped backwards, so he could turn his body to look at her but still continue towards their goal.

"Really? Not your own?" Surprised that he would assume a woman would be reading the newspapers. Well, at least his newspaper. There were society papers that most of the ton read avidly every week. The Times was a different sort of paper and instead covered more than just what happened in Londinium.

She replied honestly, "I have trouble keeping up with the scientific journals that I don't have time for newspapers." Thomas shrugged it off and spun back around in time to open the door to another room. This one had shelves up to the ceiling and the manoeuvring space between the shelves was only accomplished by stepping sideways.

He asked, "Do you know when this picture of the peeler was put into the paper?"

"No, but I assume it was when the metropolitan police were formed. Three, four years ago."

"That is a big range. But I'll check it out." He side stepped a couple of shelves and muttered to himself, reading the labels as he went. He stopped halfway down one shelf and bounced on his toes, twiddling his fingers in the air as he searched for the correct box. He pulled one down and passed it to her before going for a few more.

With the five boxes in hand they went to a table set up near the door. Thomas worked quickly and lifted out one plate at a time. He squinted before discarding it. Asking as he worked, "I didn't expect a peeler to read scientific journals. Are they useful? In your job I mean." He kept his eyes on the plates as he checked each one over.

"Very. The other day I was reading about fireworks from Hun." She resisted the urge to look over his shoulder while he checked.

"How would fireworks help peelers?" He finished one box and pushed it aside. Dragging the second one to him and leaving a clear streak in the dust on the desk. He was well informed if he was familiar enough with fireworks that he didn't ask what they were.

"We could create light and call for help. They might be useful in a riot situation," she speculated off the top of her head as she really hadn't intended for the conversation to go anywhere.

"So, will we see fireworks anytime soon?" The newspaper man asked curious. Larkin snorted. Rayne shot a sideways glance at Larkin, glad when he didn't add anything more. Thomas might be helping them but he also worked in a newspaper. If he thought what they said was newsworthy, he would print it without qualms.

"One day. Testing would have to be done first to make sure they are safe," she prevaricated instead. Thomas glanced at them.

He read the look on Larkin's face and said simply, "So never then, eh?" He didn't wait for an answer but went back to looking through the plates.

He finished the second and the third box. "You didn't tell me what you needed the plate for."

"Are you fishing for a story, Mr Barnes?" She smiled as he was a pleasant man to banter with.

He corrected her, "Thomas, thank you. Mr Barnes is my father." He shuddered dramatically. He finished up and said, "No peelers, I'm afraid. We just have some lewd graphics of people committing crimes but no peelers." He stacked up the boxes and wedged past them. He flashed her a grin when it meant pressing his body against her own. She stepped back to give him as much room as possible. He saw the move and his face dropped. He might be pleasant to talk with but that didn't mean she wanted to press her body against his.

She muttered a thank you and left while he put everything away. Larkin asked, "You don't seriously think you will find the image the tavern keeper saw? Not all newspapers keep their plates. Some have even ceased to exist."

She shrugged. It didn't harm them either. It didn't help that they didn't have any other leads.

Chapter Thirteen

The hesitation of Lady Pembroke when they were announced was telling. Rayne's mother obviously had not informed the woman that she would be attending with her daughter. Before Lady Pembroke could revoke her invitation, Rayne's mother flounced in and spread her skirts and took a seat opposite Lady Pembroke. Lady Pembroke opened her mouth to protest but must have considered the fact that Lady Ancaster was a duchess and her teeth clacked together as she swallowed whatever she was going to say. Rayne could feel some pity for the woman as she knew just how stubborn her mother could be.

Lady Ancaster flapped a hand at Rayne who found a seat on the other side of the room. Chairs shifted as people tried to get farther away from her. One person didn't move. Sir Laurie. He flashed her a cruel grin. "I see you are an accessory today."

Rayne laid her hands in her lap and ignored the comment. She was here for her mother and from experience she knew silence was the better part of valour.

Rayne curled her hands in her lap. Her metal hand half hidden under the pale-yellow glove, on her opposite hand, that matched her light-coloured dress. When she wasn't in her uniform, it was her habit to wear something that made her feel amazing. No stays or corsets, instead perfectly tailored gowns. Today she wore a one-piece dress with a drawstring waist. The skirt ended at her calf-high boots in light tanned leather.

Sir Laurie tried again. "Don't you find these things tedious?"

Rayne had a choice. Sit there in silence and be very bored or engage with Sir Laurie even if the conversation made her feel like taking a bath afterwards. Boredom was never her first choice. "Sometimes, when I have to talk to people with a mean core who find insulting others second nature, I find these outings very tedious."

He didn't seem slighted that she had implied he was mean and instead shrugged. "It is more about political expedience. I am an influential person after all." He cocked an eyebrow. It was worse when the person she wanted to insult already acknowledged that they were odious. But he also wasn't wrong.

"I'm aware of that. On the surface I look like someone who has lowered themselves to having an actual trade. But you forget that the highest-ranking nobles are those with ties to the dragons and dragons like noblemen who have a trade. It makes us unique."

He snorted. "You think your appendage will make you desirable to the dragon. He doesn't take anything unique. You know that woman he married. Well, she was a commoner. A nobody." Spitting with the vehemence of his words.

Rayne's mind went sharp. The anger in Sir Laurie's voice meant his association with Eleanor was personal. The only people from this layer of society to have met the women were her victims.

Rayne turned in her seat then stopped herself. She didn't want to reveal to Sir Laurie that she was interested in the answer. "Did you know Eleanor?"

Sir Laurie grimaced revealing his teeth. "That whore was beneath my concern." Rayne would take that as a yes.

Rayne narrowed her eyes and dug a little deeper. "Interesting, as you were Governor when she married the dragon. You would have been at the same balls. Surely you would have met."

"They were married less than a week. She only attended one ball. In this gaudy gown and dripping in jewellery."

"Jewellery the dragon had given her." Her tone digging into his pride. "Did you ever give her jewellery?"

He fidgeted, agitated by the conversation. Smoothing his fingers over his facial hair. "She sold my grandmother's brooch. Can you believe that?" He paled when he realised what he had revealed.

Rayne asked, "So were you aware she was a conman?"

His voice tipped towards being a little too loud for the polite conversation allowed in sitting room. "A conman? No, she was a…A conman? Really?"

"Yes, her partner was Sebastian. They were lovers and conned people out of as much wealth as possible. It is amazing what you can find out gossiping at an inn." Sir Laurie gaped. His pale skin flushed with embarrassment.

He tried to recover and snapped, "A great deduction, officer. I've never had a great regard for Robert's men. I think I might have to change my mind."

"Is that because of our wit or because some of us are not as honourable as you are?" She wasn't ashamed to throw herself into the mire that were her colleagues.

Sir Laurie sniffed. "I'd say your wit but I know your father would have made sure you were well educated. A complete waste in a female." His insult delivered awkwardly, he stumbled to his feet just as ungraceful as his words. He muttered an excuse of a meeting he had forgotten. The rest of the ladies and gentlemen looked confused but didn't stop Sir

Laurie from leaving. Lady Ancaster narrowed her eyes at Rayne who gave an innocent shrug. It was never a good sign when men desperately tried to escape.

K atherine wore an oversized leather apron that was folded at the bottom and pegged to keep it rolled up. This was essential as the apron was long enough to get under her feet. Katherine also wore leather gloves that were a size too big and she left her hands held up so they wouldn't slip off. At least this was the way Rayne found her sister.

Rayne said from the doorway to the basement room, "I thought you were going to start with animals." This was said because on the table in the middle of the room was a body of a man covered by an old sheet.

Katherine flashed her a grin and said, "I got lucky. One of dad's contacts said they had a body of a murderer that they were willing to sell."

Katherine waved a hand at the body. Her exuberance at the opportunity had her bouncing on her toes. "He has tattoos all over his body. He was a pirate, apparently. He is too dead to try to bring back to life but I'll be able to see where everything is inside the body. Maybe figure out what everything does."

Rayne shook her head at the obvious glee in her sister's voice. She was used to bodies but even she didn't get excited over cutting one open to see what was inside. Approaching the table, she looked down at the man. He had scars and looked like a wax model rather than a ruthless pirate.

Katherine asked, "Will you help? I can't let the servants see this. Dad is pretending it is for Everett to study medicine but the servants would know that was baloney so they can't help."

Rayne looked around and saw several sets of gloves laid out on a table to the side. Her sister had come prepared. She found one to go over her hand and tucked a cloth in her pocket to clean off her mechanical hand when this was all done. Together they moved tables and things into place so Katherine could place the organs into containers.

Rayne asked while they were setting buckets around the table, "Would you consider chemistry a hobby or a lesser science?"

Katherine grunted as she shifted a table closer and stood back to eye it. "Hardly. There is a lot you can do with chemicals. Are you talking about the dragon?"

Rayne eyed her sister curious how she had jumped to that conclusion even if it was correct. "Why would you say that?"

"Only a dragon would consider chemistry a lesser science. They are physicists. Anything that gets icky is considered lesser to them."

Rayne eyed the multitude of buckets and pans and knew this would get messy very soon and very quickly. She wondered what Victor would think of it all.

"He has a lab, so obviously he doesn't think that. What is the difference anyway?" She grunted, as the heavy basin she grabbed looked lighter than it actually was. Bending her knees, she tried again and shifted it to where it was needed while her sister answered her question.

"Most dragons only work with things at their smallest. Chemistry in comparison would be crude. Like painting with your fingers instead of a paintbrush."

"Victor isn't crude." Rayne blushed at her quick defence of the dragon. No one would believe she had no feelings for the dragon if she said things like that.

Thankfully, her sister was oblivious. Katherine finished setting up and picked up a small knife. She frowned at her gloves and then made a choice and took them off. She grinned when she handled the small knife. "I wouldn't call Victor crude either but he is nostalgic. Chemistry and biology would be where the dragons started." So much for her sister not noticing as she came back to the conversation as if she hadn't been quiet for a couple of moments.

"Biology?" Rayne asked though she was pretty sure she knew the answer. Acting dumb usually got interesting titbits from her sister.

Katherine motioned to the body on the table. "Study of life. The dragons would consider this barbaric. They would be able to just look at the body and know where all the organs are. They would also be able to tell what killed the man." She waved towards the neck where the dark bruises where the hangman's rope had strangled the life out of the man was visible.

Her sister swam in waters that Rayne didn't and therefore knew different things to what she did. "What do you mean?"

"To be able to manipulate something you have to be able to observe it. They don't see it with their eyes but rather feel where everything is and what it is made of. Dragons would make great detectives."

Katherine cut into the body and Rayne found herself looking away as the skin split way too easily under the sharp blade.

Katherine said, "You can go now. I'll be at this for hours." Rayne took the excuse and left. Scrubbing her mechanical hand more than was truly needed when she stopped at the washstand in her room.

Chapter Fourteen

Larkin lurked at the door to the press while Rayne looked through a stack of plates. He had stopped helping her look for peelers in the plates two newspapers before. Rayne wasn't sure if he thought the whole task frivolous or if he worried they would succeed and uncover a peeler as the suspect for Sebastian's murder.

He had been inordinately pleased when Markim had ended up dead rather than her having to arrest him. Rayne had apologised when she had taken in all the factors. He might be tarred with the same brush if anything happened to her. His silence had been more support than she had expected.

That made this hunt problematic for him. It was almost like Larkin didn't want to uncover the killer but was also drawn to solving the case at the same time.

Realising she had been staring at the same plate for over a minute she shook herself. The clacks of the press in the other room kept her aware of the time that passed, constant they had invaded even her thoughts. She sighed and put aside the plate and picked up the next one.

Larkin asked, "What would you do if it was Lord Rowan?" The question surprised Rayne but showed that Larkin had been wrestling with this longer than she had.

She hadn't considered that. All she had thought was no matter who it was deserved justice. She did hesitate when she thought of Lord Rowan possibly being the killer.

"I doubt it is him. He is too honourable." It would break her mother's heart to even think of her childhood friend being capable of killing someone and then framing the dragon for it.

Eerily contradicting her comments to Sir Laurie and his narrow-minded view of people Larkin said, "Most of the peelers are. But there is a point that can push even a good man into doing evil. Maybe they thought they were doing the right thing. What if he knew more about the matter and was trying to save someone? We don't know enough to just hunt down whoever it was with prejudice."

Rayne wasn't so sure of the other peelers and their honour. Some had propositioned her or revealed their hatred of women by a word and by ostracising her. None of those traits would have made her think they were honourable. Larkin would see it differently as he would have only seen the side of them that spent their days helping others. He would assume all the men were like him just because they did the same thing.

Rayne stopped at a plate and said, "I was thinking more on the lines of being highly cautious instead of pursuing anything with prejudice. I don't want to be killed because I brought in the murderer of a conman and his lover. Even when I know the killer, I'll probably keep it between us until I can find more. Besides, I don't think anyone will be able to do anything about it at the Metropolitan police. After all, they knew Markim was a blackmailer and all they did was fire him. I need a more permanent solution for our killer for us to be safe." She had taken to wearing the flint lock her mother had given her. It even glistened with hours of polishing. Fields would be proud of her.

She held the plate up to Larkin and asked, "Who does this look like?" Larkin narrowed his eyes as he looked at the plate.

"Maynes? I didn't know he had glasses?" He took the plate from her hands to have a closer look. Taking it over to the door and the light outside.

"He only wears them when he is reading." She revealed as Larkin never came to report to the man so wouldn't have seen him poring over the files with a set of spectacles on his nose.

Larkin shook his head. "Maynes is way too straight laced to kill anyone." Like that had ever stopped someone who had a reason to kill. Besides, she was pretty sure he was the one who had spread the rumours that Victor was a suspect in Sebastian case even though there was no evidence. If he was the real killer, then him turning the blame on to another made sense. Even him assigning her to the case made sense. He didn't have much respect for her and her abilities. He had probably hoped she wouldn't find any evidence. They hadn't really, not enough to tie Maynes to the murder in any case. Just the publican's word and they didn't even know if this was the image he remembers from the newspapers.

"He is the only peeler we have seen in the newspapers." They had searched almost all of them, so she could say that with some authority.

Larkin was still sceptical. "That we know of. The other plates could have been lost or the newspaper no longer around. You don't know this is the only picture of a policeman to be in the papers."

Rayne shrugged but the more she let this clue sit inside her head the more it made sense. But she would keep it to herself for the time being. Now she would have to convince the newspaper that she could have the plate.

Rayne let Larkin think he had won the battle when he made her take the plate to the innkeeper to see if he recognised the image. She would have done that anyway in the hope the image would help the innkeeper remember other details that could be helpful. Besides, there was no way she would be going after one of the heads of the metropolitan police force without solid, irrefutable proof.

Smoke curled over the tops of the buildings and flavoured the air. Men ran past them with whatever container they could carry. The roar of the fire became more evident as they turned the corner. People passed over buckets and containers down a line from a fountain two streets down.

They didn't bother with the building itself but rather the buildings next to it. Frantically making sure the fire didn't spread to the vulnerable structures.

Rayne stared in disbelief as she watched the Maiden's Hare sag and collapse under the inferno. Sparks burst into light then faded as they used up all their energy.

Larkin asked, "Suspicious. Someone covering their tracks?"

"I hope not. Because that would mean they are still one step ahead of us and we are running out of leads." It bothered her. She hadn't spoken with anyone of what they were looking for. As far as Maynes knew they were working on new cases and that the murder had been shelved until new evidence was uncovered. Larkin was the only one who knew they were still looking and he was so reluctant to speak with her about the whole thing she knew he wouldn't bring it up with Rosie let alone one of the other Bobbies at the Yard.

The killer could be panicking but it was weeks since the murder, it was unlikely that was his thought process. On the other hand, it could all be an accident. But it just didn't feel right to Rayne.

She searched the crowd to see if she could find the innkeeper or the man who had been helpful last time. Hopefully, they could salvage this in some way. Before they could search the whole crowd, they were dragooned in to helping with the buckets of water, their uniforms too distinct for them to pretend they were civilians. Besides in situations like this everyone put in a hand. The danger of the city burning was too high of a risk for people to stand by and do nothing.

It was dark by the time they headed back to the Yard. Though she wasn't sure what the hour was. Covered in soot, her arms ached from passing over buckets of water. One thing about putting out the fire, they had been around long enough to know the innkeeper had been inside his establishment when it went up and he hadn't made it out.

Exhausted, she resisted dragging her feet as she stepped over the threshold of the office foyer. A runner dashed in front of her and then out the door almost tumbling her over in the process. She called out a sharp, "Hey." but the boy was already well down the block and out of earshot. She turned back inside too tired to be even mad at the boy.

There was a commotion inside as well. Officers huddled in groups and gossiped like mama's sizing up men for their daughters. While others rushed from place to place in seeming random fashion.

Charles Rowan appeared at the top of the stairs and used his baton to tap on the railing to get everyone's attention. Everyone silenced and stood where they were to hear what Lord Rowan had to say. "The former Governor of London, Sir Laurie, was murdered last night. We will all be working on this and we will have meetings starting in an hour so we can catch this criminal."

The air left her lungs. It was clear everyone already knew this news.

Charles rattled off the names of officers who would be in charge of different aspects of the case. He then disappeared back into his offices.

Fields spotted her standing like a stunned mullet at the door and barked, "At it, men." Startled to be lumped in with the others Rayne moved before she even thought of what she could do to help with the investigation.

Larkin broke off from her side to join one of the huddled groups. When he returned, he said, "He was found dead in his own home. Bashed in the head with a paper weight."

The circumstances sounded surprisingly similar to Markim's death. Another panicked attack to cover tracks? Sir Laurie also recently found out that Eleanor was a conman. Had he been working with someone? Someone he had revealed to that he now knew Eleanor was a conman. Rayne winced as she remembered bringing up the fact she had gained this knowledge from talking to people at the inn. The killer must have gotten that out of Sir Laurie before he died. That was why they had taken out the inn even though it was weeks after Sebastian's death.

———

When people started looking into Sir Laurie's death, they discovered he hated Victor. A long-standing rivalry that many had witnessed. Then the papers announced a connection between Sir Laurie and Victor. His wife Eleanor had been Sir Laurie's mistress. That put Victor back up to the top of the list of possible murderers for not only Sir Laurie but also Eleanor as people started to speculate that he had discovered this and killed her in a jealous rage. They retroactively assigned to Sir Laurie his reasons for pardoning Sebastian because of his suspicions. The newspapers speculated that the dragon had only returned to silence Sir Laurie who had new evidence. None of the newspapers asked her what her thoughts were on the case even though she was the one investigating Sebastian's death.

Victor was clever enough to keep a low profile and he stopped going to balls and outings. A small group of protestors set themselves outside his house. Not quite a mob but certainly unsettling.

Rayne didn't worry that Victor behind the death of Sir Laurie. Like her speculation that a dragon would merely eat any offending human he managed to kill, she didn't think he was passionate enough over Eleanor or Sebastian to have killed Sir Laurie so many years later.

The newspapers made links as well. After all, Sir Laurie had Sebastian pardoned years before. How they found out Sebastian had once worked for Sir Laurie was interesting but none of the papers connected the dots to figure out the con Sebastian and Eleanor had been involved in. Even if they weren't into lurid speculation about the relationship between Eleanor and Victor.

The attacks started to happen the next night. Random people on the street were attacked. Robbed and beaten up. When asked who did it, they all said it was the dragon.

Rayne had tried to see Victor but he had been scarce at his residence as well. She wondered if this would draw the dragons from Europe. They wouldn't tolerate one of their own breaking the treaty and they would also not tolerate humans putting to death a dragon.

When a dragon from Europe arrived, a ball was thrown in his honour. Even Rayne managed to get an invite despite the result of her last outing with a dragon present. Maybe they thought she would be able to get the dragon to reveal his true colours.

Lady Beechworth said by Rayne's side, "I see you went with the gold." Rayne had returned home too late to have a say in the gown. Her mother had put it out for her. She would have preferred something that didn't show so much skin. Her arms were bare and the single gold glove on her one hand made her other look like she was wearing a matching glove on her mechanical side. That was the only reason she had gone along with the dress in the first place. But it also showed her collarbone and the puff sleeve engulfed her shoulders. It also didn't cover up the brace that held her hand in place.

The boat cut collar revealed too much of her cleavage for comfort. Her bobby uniform usually covered everything but this outfit revealed just how endowed she was.

"It isn't for the dragons," she reassured Lady Beechworth.

"There is only one dragon here tonight." Lady Beechworth motioned to the other side of the ballroom. There were two people standing alone. Unlike before there were no tittering women and the ambience was certainly hostile.

The couple stood together oblivious to the cold shoulder of those around them. The woman was dark-haired but otherwise non-descript and most likely the dragon's mate. In Rayne's mind she had lumped the woman with the dragon. She shouldn't as the woman wouldn't have the same powers but it was automatic as the two worked in sync with each other so seamlessly. They were true partners.

"What can you tell me about them?" Rayne studied the male dragon. He was large and did not seem very cheery. The woman kept up most of the conversation while he listened with a slight frown.

"They are fixers," Lady Beechworth said after a slight shrug of her shoulder. Rayne snorted at the concept. The woman, in a beautiful blue gown, was a delicate flower against the wall that was the dragon.

Lady Beechworth frowned at her dismissiveness. "I'm serious. Whenever there is trouble, they send those two. There was a man hunting dragons when I was a little girl. He ran here when the dragons started hunting him. These two were the ones to chase him down and put him out of his misery."

Rayne glanced at Lady Beechworth. She was well into her fifties. If she remembered these two from when she was a little girl then the woman was much older than Rayne had expected.

Rayne asked, "Dragon mates live as long as dragons?" She gathered from the anecdote.

"Yes. These two are the most obvious as they go all over the place and mix with humans. Most of the others who mate with dragons eventually move away from society. I think it would be hard to keep watching all your family die."

Rayne had to agree but she now thought more about Victor's offer of marriage. So far, no dragons had died from old age though she doubted anyone would know if they had. Dragons were notorious for keeping their own secrets. She could see why women would suffer a kind of slavery to a dragon if they could stay young for a very long time.

Rayne pointed out the lack of sycophants and asked, "Is Society aware that they are fixers." That might explain the lack of people courting the dragon but it could also do with the newspapers or the fact that he was already taken.

Lady Beechworth gave a short, "Ha. Those silly people wouldn't know if a snake was sleeping in their beds. No, those are the ones who supported Sir Laurie when he was alive. His death has given them a martyr to back. They want dragons out of England. Anyway, they can."

Rayne took more notice of the people who glared at the two. She knew some people weren't keen on dragons having any say in the government but she hadn't realised the feeling had permeated so much of the upper echelons of society. Much of society had their positions of power because of their connections to dragons. It seemed counter-productive to bite the hand that fed them.

With that in mind she said to Lady Beechworth, "I think I might just introduce myself."

CHAPTER FIFTEEN

The door opened, bathing the empty street with candlelight and Rayne caught her breath. Maynes tugged his coat closer around him against the cold night. He glanced around looking for anyone on the streets before he stepped away from his doorstep.

Rayne peeled out of the small shadows she had been hiding in and followed him as he made his way through the streets of Londinium. Moving from shadow to shadow in case he glanced behind him.

She had been following him for two nights. Hoping he was the one behind the attacks and that it wasn't someone else that was trying to frame Victor. That would be in the realm of impossible or unlikely. Unfortunately, she didn't have any evidence it was Maynes who was the killer or the new 'dragon' attacker that was being reported in the newspapers.

Maynes moved down the street as if on a mission. Giving her hope he was on his way to further blacken Victor's name. It was disappointing when he stopped at a theatre two blocks over. She didn't go inside as the lights would make it easier to spot her.

Instead, she found a hiding spot in the shadows of a highly decorated building. She had a good view of the entrance and settled in to wait.

She almost jumped out of her skin when Victor said just behind her, "Now what is a pretty girl like you doing out in the middle of the night on Londinium's streets?"

She turned to glare at Victor. "I can ask you the same thing."

He patted his hair and said, "I do have nice hair but I wouldn't go so far as to call me pretty. Handsome maybe."

Rayne turned back to watch the theatre. "I don't have time for this, Victor." She had no idea how he had found her and assumed it was another dragon ability she didn't know of.

He leaned on the wall next to her, close enough that she could feel the heat coming off his body. "Oh, are we on first name basis again?"

She almost asked him how he found her but she dreaded the answer. Besides it wasn't that important. Instead she said, "Being annoying is not a great way to court someone."

"Courting? That is better than where we were before."

She glanced over her shoulder and asked, "What are you even doing out. I thought you were hiding from the mobs."

"Funnily enough when the temperature is low the mob seems to disappear. There was a single diligent bigot at my door this evening and it didn't take much to sneak past him. He still thinks I'm at home and he is standing watch with his pitchfork and torch."

She sighed at his dramatic portrayal of the few people who staked out his home. They were mostly annoying rather than dangerous.

Changing the subject, she announced, "I met another dragon."

He stepped in closer and asked intensely, "Who?"

A smiled slipped onto her lips for a moment at his obvious jealousy.

"Lady Beechworth calls them fixers."

He relaxed. Taking a step back. "Oh, that is only Harlen."

"So, she was right, they really are fixers." Rayne had spoken with them at the ball. Most people had watched on nervously in case another full-sized dragon happened to transform again in the ballroom. Some had been disappointed when nothing had happened. Maybe she had been invited because of what had happened at the last ball. Harlen had been on his best behaviour and had asked questions about her investigation into Eleanor and Sebastian's deaths. They revealed they were more concerned about Victor as a suspect in Sebastian's death than in the more recent death of Sir Laurie. The timeline made more sense as they had arrived almost as the reports in the newspapers had started. They must have already been on their way.

She had been frank as possible. Her godfather would have wanted her to be transparent but a casual comment had revealed that Maynes had been keeping them in the dark. That was when she had decided to follow Maynes. With the death of the innkeeper she couldn't use the plate she had taken from the newspaper. But it didn't change the possibility that he had been having a meal with Sebastian just before his death. Or the possibility Sir Laurie had revealed the truth of Eleanor to Maynes. Sealing his own fate. Frustratingly, she had nothing tangible to take to Charles.

Relaxed, Victor tucked his hands into his pockets. Probably to keep his hands warm as the temperature at night was chilly at best but it was clear he wasn't intimidated by the idea of the fixers who were here to investigate him. "Yeah, they work for the Emperor," He confirmed for her.

She frowned as she glanced at him over her shoulder. She kept her focus on the theatre so it was hard to see his expressions as they spoke. "We have an Empress at the moment. You dragons really do get out of touch with reality," Rayne corrected him.

"Oh, I meant Emperor." This made her half turn to see if he was serious. He added, "The dragon Emperor."

"You mean he is still alive." She had heard that William the Conqueror's father was still around. He had been the instigator of the treaty between dragons and humans. Mostly to keep his descendants safe. It had heralded a time of peace between dragons and humans in Europe that had allowed them to flourish as a civilisation. She had thought he was a myth, almost.

"Yes, no one has put him out of his misery yet though I don't see how Harlen puts up with him. He can be so insufferable."

"Who is Harlen?" She didn't mean as a dragon but rather his position in the organisation of dragons. There were certainly gaps in her understanding of the hierarchy.

"He is the Emperor's brother. Was Lala there?" Rayne had liked Lala. She had been pleasant and sincere which made Rayne instantly fond of her.

"Yes. She seemed nice."

Victor snorted. "To you maybe. She scares the bejeebus out of me."

She chuckled at the thought of the woman in the elegant gown scaring a dragon but he grew serious.

"She is a dragon hunter." Victor's eyes warmed as he teased her with new information.

"Nooo. Wait Lala...that is a Romany name." She snuck another glance back at him.

He nodded, agreeing with her deduction. "Yes, and the Romany took in the hunters when they were made outlaws."

Her mind wandered back to her meeting with Lala. There had been no evidence that she was powerful enough to kill a dragon. But that was the point of dragon hunters, to take out dragons. Rayne had thought they were extinct. Dragons had left them out of the treaty and so they were fair game for any dragon.

"A dragon hunter? Interesting. I can see why they are sent in to fix things then. Harlen would have the political clout because of his brother and she would be able to kill any dragon who was trouble," Rayne thought out loud.

"Oh, Harlen has taken out a few of our brethren. Besides, he doesn't play politics. Only his brother does, he has a tendency to stick his nose into places it shouldn't be. Harlen plays a buffer between the Empress and the Emperor. Stops him from interfering too much." The fact that dragons still called him Emperor showed just how successful Harlen had been. At least the humans hadn't figured out yet that he was playing puppet master. She wasn't sure herself how she felt about that.

"Do you think he has come for you?" she asked wondering if his calm was because he hadn't gathered that Harlen was here to put Victor out of his misery if he really was a killer. Victor snorted at the idea.

"No, I think he is here to sort out the newspapers. Good riddance. I have no idea where they have been getting their stories." From what Harlen had been asking she didn't think he would do anything about the papers. He was playing nice with the authorities and to get the newspapers sorted would take some draconian measures, pun intended.

"Most likely from the Yard," she answered honestly. She had been reading the newspapers herself and there were details about the attacks that were in her reports and nowhere else. Between her and Larkin the only other person who knew what were in those reports was Maynes.

"You?" his voice not serious as he lightly accused her.

"I should be insulted. No, I think the killer is an officer and they are framing you. The articles in the newspapers are on purpose. Your trial is being held right now and the jury is the public." She wasn't any more specific. Besides he would figure it out when he saw who she was following tonight. She still didn't feel confident to accuse a fellow officer of murder when all she had was speculation. Not even circumstantial evidence.

"That doesn't sound pleasant." His voice more amused than upset over the newspapers. She wasn't so sure he should be so cavalier over the impact of public opinion.

"Then it is a good thing that your dragon fixer is getting involved." Though if Harlen did try to stop the newspapers, he would only make the situation worse. She didn't think Lala or Harlen were the type to add fire to the situation so she wasn't really worried that would happen. It would mean the newspapers would continue to write articles about the vices of dragons and Victor in particular.

Victor got speculative over Harlen's presence. "Maybe. If he goes with what the Yard tells him, he might think I really did kill Eleanor." Except that the Yard had gone silent on Harlen. Now she saw this could be a good thing as it had opened up for her to tell Harlen the truth behind the investigation. That particular strategy had certainly backfired on Maynes.

It sounded like Harlen had been a fixer for the Emperor for a while, so he might have been involved back when Eleanor had died. Curious she asked, "Did they not investigate back when she died? Surely there would have been more upset then?"

"Yes and no. I went to Europe and explained myself. They were satisfied when I didn't show any mating marks." He offered his arm to her. Pushing up a sleeve to show his pale skin was clear.

"Mating marks?" She had heard of them but like with her sister she liked to play dumb and see what little nuggets of information she might collect from the dragon.

Victor didn't disappoint and explained, "When dragons get married, they brand each other. If they get divorced, they disappear. The brands disappeared the same time that Eleanor did. If Eleanor was still my mate when she died I would have still had the brands."

She hadn't realised dragons could get divorced. "She divorced you. Isn't that difficult?" The divorces she had heard of amongst humans was usually drawn out and painful. With all the couple's dirty laundry put on display for everyone who cared to gossip. But then the ton were not kind to those that didn't manage to achieve the perfection society required.

"Not for dragons. She made a choice and renounced me and that was all that was needed. I didn't even need to be there for it. She must have renounced me speaking with someone else as she never admitted it to me personally. I was blindsided. I went home to find the place almost completely empty. She'd had movers come in and empty it in an afternoon while I was with the Governor." Now that was something she hadn't known.

"Sir Laurie?" Her eyes were on the theatre but her mind was turning over the new information. Eleanor would have known she had cut ties with the dragon as well when her own brand disappeared. Had she waited to be away from Victor to do that or had she, like Rayne, not known about the ease of dragon divorce and divorced him unknowingly. That could have put a wrinkle in the two cons' plans. She still didn't know how Maynes played into all of this but it added a new facet to her investigation. Had Eleanor and Sebastian ended their part of the plan too early?

Victor explained more about his relationship with Sir Laurie without her having to do more than a vague prompt. "Yeah, we weren't seeing eye to eye and I was in negotiations with him about changing laws."

"Wait, laws?" She half turned again. More information she hadn't known. It seemed the dragons' influence wasn't just coming from the Emperor of dragons himself but all his people.

"Yes, my role here is to help guide the humans to a more egalitarian way of life. We can't move too fast or you get upset so we wheedle and whine until things change." She was going to ask him to explain when the door to the theatre opened and cut off her thought.

She frowned. It was way too early for the show to be over. Maynes slipped out and closed the door behind him. He looked around but didn't spot them in the shadows.

"Why now?" She asked the air.

Victor answered anyway, "His alibi."

She swore softly under her breath as she moved to follow Maynes. He was up to no good if he needed to make sure that people thought he was at the theatre when whatever he planned went down.

Victor skipped to keep up with her as she had surprised him with her sudden movement. He didn't speak which she appreciated as they both slipped from shadow to shadow as they followed Maynes.

Maynes didn't travel at a steady pace, instead he stopped occasionally to add or take something away from his outfit. He moved under a street lantern revealing his new appearance.

Victor swore. "He looks like me."

Victor never kept up with fashion and wore outfits out a few seasons and therefore very distinct. Maynes was even wearing the same waistcoat Victor was currently wearing. Maynes had also donned a wig to hide his own pale locks to match Victor's much darker hair.

Rayne had been pretty sure Maynes had been behind the rumours of attacks by Victor but she hadn't been sure how he had achieved it. She had thought he had merely paid the people to say they were attacked by Victor but this was even more sinister as those people would swear to their graves it was the dragon who attacked them. She still didn't know Maynes' motivations or why he hated dragons. It was curious that he had similar views to dragons as the late Sir Laurie.

Maynes stopped outside another theatre, forcing them to duck into an alley. They looked around the edge of the building. Maynes disappointingly didn't do anything. He just stood there outside of the theatre. She held her breath waiting for him to attack or something.

Victor interrupted the tension by asking, "Are we courting? We are on an outing."

The comment so out of left field that she answered with a snap to her voice. "I'd hardly call this romantic."

There was a smile in his voice as he added, "Maybe to others but this is your passion." She glanced back at him surprised by his insight.

She rewarded him by being honest. "I won't ever marry. A husband would require me to give up my work and I don't want that."

He didn't seem perturb by her announcement and instead asked, "But do you still want children?"

That was unlikely to ever be one of her choices. "If I could find a man willing to treat me like an equal instead of a brood mare, sure I wouldn't mind having children. I just don't see how they'd fit into my life at the moment."

His voice grew deeper as he stated simply, "Acceptable."

She frowned at him, not sure what he meant by that. But she had to turn back to Maynes who was making his move. Someone had left the theatre a little ahead of everyone else so they were alone. Maynes followed them as they headed for the main street where they would be able to call for a hansom cab.

Rayne tugged on Victor's coat to urge him to follow her as she dashed across the street. She heard the scream and added a little more energy to her step. Dragging her skirts up so she could run faster. Victor passed her as he didn't have the impediments of cloth.

She muttered a long-worn curse over women's clothing and got to the street in time to see Maynes running and Victor crouched over the man. She hesitated at the tableau but Victor called out, "I've got this. Get after him." She saw a flash of blue light as Victor pulled something out of his collection for the injuries the man had suffered.

She hitched up her skirts higher but Maynes was already gaining distance on her. When her lungs started to burn and Maynes ducked down an alley and then out of sight she stopped chasing him.

She wished she could have caught him in the act but having to live with just knowing she had been right about the attacks reported in the newspapers would have to do. Victor at least was not guilty on this charge.

The rest were still up for debate as far as the Yard was concerned. She trudged back towards Victor and the large crowd that had gathered around him. Her breath still laboured she came to a stop. The crowd seethed with tension. Steeling herself, she approached. Shoving at people became useless as no one would move out of the way.

The theatre show must have finished, spilling the crowd onto the street in time to see the attack. Unfortunately, they wouldn't have seen Maynes. She tried elbowing her way through but the jeers and the crowd kept her back. Someone shoved her and she landed on her rear. She could have fought the crowd more to get to the victim but it would mean revealing she was a bobby and the feel of the crowd made her weary. Not all peelers were appreciated by the public and she was alone.

Victor, as a dragon, could easily escape so she didn't worry about him. Making her way to the edges of the crowd she waited for it to disperse. Instead of dispersing, the crowd started to move in a concerted direction. She climbed a short wall to see if she could see the centre of the crowd. Her heart dropped when she saw Victor unconscious and dragged between two burly men.

CHAPTER SIXTEEN

Raynes slapped the newspaper on her father's desk.

"They arrested him. That man would be dead if it wasn't for Victor but they arrested him and made all these silly accusations."

Her father looked up from the book he was reading and glanced between her and the newspaper. He raised an eyebrow asking for permission. She waved for him to pick it up. The article was accompanied by a dragon fighting a knight. Bones of past victims scattered around the brave knight. She had seen this image before in many of the newspapers. It seemed they shared plates as well as stories.

Dragons hadn't been enemies of humans for centuries but whenever humans wanted to vilify them, they would remind people of the dragon's past or that they were invaders. Dragons were refugees. Their own planet was no longer habitable. Earth had been their only option.

Her father asked, "Are you going to go to the trial?"

"There won't be space and I'm working on that day." Her voice revealing that she already felt defeated. She had no control over the magistrate and Maynes would have been the one to report on the case findings. She knew from the work in the newspapers that he would probably have Victor accused with all the murders. Eleanor, Sebastian and probably Sir Laurie. Though she doubted he would lump in Markim. That was a loose end she could still explore if she could only find the material he was using to blackmail his victims with.

Her father raised an eyebrow. "Charles will be there, why don't you call on him and see if you can be his escort or something." She didn't like using her godfather for things like this. It wasn't essential for her to see the trial. It was a forgone conclusion that he would be convicted. The newspapers were already speculating on the date of the execution.

Her father finished reading the article and asked, "How did they get so many details about the attack? It is rare they are this effuse on the actual event."

Rayne grunted. "The real attacker is the one speaking to the press."

Her father leant back in his seat. "I think you have to go to the trial. If there is a conspiracy against Victor, then they might reveal more at the trial." She winced. From her father's words he expected her to exonerate Victor after his death.

Feeling powerless was her least favourite emotion and it made her sharp. "It won't change anything." She sniffed as she held back tears.

She knew what the outcome of the trial would be and it wasn't going to be a good ending for Victor. With Harlen here they might intervene but unlikely. It would cause more trouble to rescue Victor from the law than it would have been to merely get rid of him if he really was the attacker.

Her father asked, "You care about him?"

She didn't want to admit her feelings as they were too raw and new. Her disability had closed the door on a relationship. To allow her heart to feel was like moving an old cart but once moving it gained momentum. "He isn't too bad for a dragon."

Her father looked thoughtful and that only worried her. She left him deep in thought. She had to find a way to save Victor. He was innocent and it was her job to make sure only the guilty paid. First, she would try her godfather but she was doubtful he would have any power in this situation. He had told her once he could do less for her now that she was an officer as he couldn't seem to favour her over the others. For this she would plead.

———

Rayne tugged at her coat as they settled into their seats in the old bailey. She was agitated as they had to wait for the other formalities before they even got to Victor's case.

Charles on the other hand was relaxed as he did these almost every other day. "It is nice to have you along, dear."

"You do know this is serious? A man's life is on the line." She had laid her problem in front of her godfather. He now knew everything she did. Even her suspicions of Maynes. He had confirmed there was little he could do. Maynes held the same amount of power as him in the police force so Charles couldn't arrest him without solid proof and even then, he would have to convince the Governor to also back the arrest warrant and conviction. They had never had someone at such a high position go rogue and there was no precedent to dealing with it.

Charles shrugged. "These things tend to iron themselves out. Especially for a dragon. I'm sure that if the Empress isn't happy with the outcome, she will step in."

His optimism annoyed her, especially since he knew how dire the situation was. "Not in time. If they sentence him to death, he will be dead before the Empress can do anything." Though she did wonder if the Emperor would something.

Charles raised an eyebrow and asked, "Tell me again why you are so sure he isn't the one that is attacking people." Her heart sunk. If he didn't believe her with just what she had seen then even with solid evidence, he might not move on it.

"I told you, I was there." Her voice low but adamant. She didn't want anyone else to hear her.

"And of course, because you are female, they don't believe you. Why didn't you take Larkin with you?" It was clearer now that Charles was aware of people's views of women and had protected her without her even realising it. Maybe he wasn't as ambivalent to the situation as she had thought but he also wasn't going to be the knight in shining armour that was going to solve all her problems. When it came to Maynes and Victor she was on her own.

She sighed and settled back into the seat. They would have to stop talking soon as the sessions started. Rayne felt a little guilty that she had left Larkin out but she didn't want him to ruin his reputation amongst the other officers if he supported her while she went on a hunt for one of their own. But she had to give Charles another reason for not including her partner.

"Larkin is seeing a lady. I didn't want to interrupt his courting for a hunch."

He hummed to himself as he thought, but he didn't divulge if he had come to a conclusion on Victor's guilt and the session started so she had to wait.

By the time it was Victor's turn to appear before court she was on the edge of the seat and her leg bounced up and down in anxious energy. Charles reached forward and rested his hand on her leg, reminding her to hide her concern. Her heels clicked on the wooden floors sharply just as Victor was guided into the room and placed in the pen.

Victor glanced around at people. They had cuffed him and placed something around his neck. She knew of these devices as there was a set in the Yard but she had never seen them even taken down, let alone used. They were supposed to keep a dragon trapped in his human form and they must work as Victor didn't walk with his usual arrogance. She would even risk saying he was scared.

Her hands clamped around her knees as she stopped herself from rushing to his defence. The magistrate called out for attention as everyone who had an excuse to be here had wheedled their way into the bailey. He droned through the accusations and when the magistrate added in Sebastian and Eleanor's deaths; she knew things were not going to go well.

The trial was less than an hour and mostly that was because people argued over how the Empress would see the outcome of the trial. The only one who had presented evidence was Maynes and there had been no counsel for Victor. He could clearly afford one but she wondered if it would have made a difference even if he had one. Everyone had convicted Victor before they had come to court.

Rayne looked around for Harlen and his dragon hunter wife, Lala. She eventually spotted them on the other side of the bailey. They must have snuck in as they were standing in the doorway. All the seats had already been taken.

Harlen stood with his arms crossed over his chest. Lala frowned at the proceedings but that could be in concentration to make out the several different conversations that took place on the floor at once. It was clear they weren't planning to make any move or give an opinion on what the Emperor of the dragons would think of the humans executing one of his own.

When Victor was convicted and sentenced to death, the air left her lungs and she felt light-headed. She had known it was coming but when the door shut on the inevitable; it crushed her.

CHAPTER EIGHTEEN

It was harder to find Harlen than she had expected. He didn't have a home in Londinuim and he hadn't been staying with Victor. Apparently, dragons were territorial and unless they were in the same collection, they never cohabitated. In the end she found Harlen staying at a posh hotel.

Nervous, she straightened her coat before she knocked on the door. The adjustment did little to put her straight as the rush to find Harlen and Lala had discombobulated her. As an afterthought she patted at her hair to make sure everything was still in place as she waited for the door to open.

Lala answered the door. Seemingly unsurprised to have a female bobby at her door, she stepped back silently inviting her inside. Lala was no longer masquerading as a lady and wore leather leggings with a multitude of weapons strapped to her.

Harlen asked, "Who is it?"

"Victor's mate." Lala called back to Harlen. Rayne had introduced herself at the ball so Lala knew her name. It bothered Rayne that she had managed to acquire a new label.

Rayne coughed. "We aren't mated." It frightened her that there was a silent 'yet' in that answer. Lala must have heard it as well as she raised her eyebrows. Rayne wasn't sure where Lala had heard that Victor had offered for her. But since their job was to investigate it gave her hope that they were good at their job.

Harlen came into the room from the dressing room. He was buttoning up his top and asked, "What does she want?"

Rayne didn't prevaricate, "We have to save Victor."

Lala sighed. Maybe she felt like Rayne, genuinely sad at the outcome of the trial and the situation they all found themselves in. "We can't. We'd love to but there has been trouble here already. The humans keep accusing us that we interfere in England too much. If we were on the continent, they wouldn't pretend and just acknowledge that they can't do anything without the dragons interfering."

Harlen let out a pleased sound and said, "You are sounding like me, love." He finished dressing and ran his hand through his hair as the entirety of his ablutions.

Lala ignored his interruption and said, "It has to be a human who interferes here."

Rayne was almost too angry to hear the undertone of Lala's words. She paced and came back a little calmer. "Are you saying I should rescue him? I would ruin my career."

Lala's eyes softened. "Is he worth it? Is a man's life worth it?"

Harlen added unhelpfully, "Dragon."

Lala flapped a hand at him to urge him to silence as she kept her gaze on Rayne.

Rayne let out a breath. "It isn't that easy."

Lala let a sad smile touch her lips. "Life is complicated." She turned to Harlen. "Do you have anything for her?"

He narrowed his eyes. "Why do you keep giving away my collection?"

Lala placed a fist on her waist and raised an eyebrow at Harlen. "Our collection. Now hand it over." If this was slavery between dragons and their mate, she could see what Victor meant when he said it was about owning each other.

Harlen sighed and a small flash of blue light revealed he had brought a small box into reality. It was decorated with carvings of the Han on the sides. He handed it to her and said, "This should be helpful. Now we must leave. We can't be here when this all goes down or they will accuse us of having a hand in it. Even if we did." Looking significantly at the box in her hands. She wondered what they had given her.

He returned to the dressing room probably to finish packing. Lala patted Rayne's hand that was around the box and said, "It will work out."

Rayne hated that Charles' sentiment was echoed when all Rayne could see was death and darkness. "I've heard that but I can't see it."

CHAPTER NINETEEN

Katherine patted the covered cart and said to Everett, "He's ready."

Katherine smiled at Rayne and said, "Don't be so worried. This will work."

Rayne had always known that when society let her down there was one bastion that never failed her. Family. She hadn't gone to her parents but instead her siblings. In this case their expertise for trouble was in need. But her family always had her back no matter how mad her plan was.

"This is crazy," Rayne countered though she was aware it was their only option if they wanted to save Victor and her career at the same time.

Everett lifted the handle of the cart and said, "Come on guys we need to be in place before the crowds appear." He started moving without waiting to see if they were ready.

Katherine stayed behind as she had a different role to play. She held the box Harlen and Lala had given her and smiled at them as Rayne and Everett went outside the gaol to where the gallows stood.

It was early. Even the bakers weren't out yet on the way to work. It could technically be considered nighttime by most people's standards. Rayne tugged her black coat close around her against the cold.

The gallows sat lonely in the courtyard outside the gaol. It was one of the few still left for the amusement of the crowds. Other gaols had started holding their executions inside their walls. The public uproar had convinced the authorities that a public execution was for the better. For Rayne it meant they had a chance to come up with an eleventh-hour rescue.

Everett crouch down by the platform of the gallows and lifted the trapdoor. He scrambled inside. Rayne hesitated but went for the cart and took out the item covered in the canvas and slid it into the gap under the gallows. Everett pulled it in, his hands the only part of him she could see in the shadows.

Rayne hid the cart in a courtyard a block over and returned to the gallows.

Everett lay on the ground with his head out of the hole. He called, "It is going to be a tight fit."

She crouched to fit in next to him. There was barely any space. They moved until the trapdoor wasn't obstructed by their bodies. It was going to be an uncomfortable stay but one necessary for their plans. Also, a lot safer to go with this than any other plan they had discussed. She had called the mission crazy but it was well thought out and all risks minimized as much as possible. It would also mean no one would know she played a part in Victor's rescue and that would mean her career was safe.

Everett asked into the silence, "Are you going to marry him?" She could have scolded him to be silent but there was no one outside who could possibly hear them yet.

"Let's rescue him first before you start planning the wedding." He chuckled at her sharp retort but kept quiet.

A while later they could hear people outside gathering around the gallows, ready for the spectacle that would happen later in the day. Rayne tugged on the collar around her neck. It was getting stuffy in the small space as the sun rose and beat on the wooden slats above. It was too tight to remove her coat so she would have to suffer the heat.

She could make out the shape of Everett on the other side of the space but the item they had dragged in here was between them and obscured him. With the lack of light, she couldn't make out his features either.

When the noise made by the crowd covered whatever noise they made, they moved the last pieces into place. They covered themselves and the item in black cloth, and shifted everything so they wouldn't be seen when the trapdoor dropped.

They had a little food but Rayne only nibbled as she knew they were going to be there for hours with no chance of privacy from her brother. There was no chance she would be able to take out time for ablutions so any amount of food was problematic.

Footsteps on the wood above them heralded that the main event was about to begin. Her heart beat so hard in her ears that she didn't hear them bringing Victor onto the platform. She jumped when the magistrate slammed a cane on the floorboards. Slapping a hand over her mouth so she didn't make a noise as the magistrate droned out the accusations against Victor.

The hangman brought Victor over the trapdoor. His frame casting gaps of shadow and light as they shifted him to where they could slip the noose around his neck. His head was covered with a hood so Rayne couldn't even try to see what he was feeling not that she could make out much with the awkward angle and obstruction of the platform.

The crowd were extraordinarily loud as they jeered. Usually it was directed towards the hangman but this time it was towards Victor.

When the hanging commenced it shocked her enough that she jerked with surprise. The trapdoor dropped and Rayne couldn't help gasping. Victor's feet came into view and flailed around.

Rayne muttered, "Now, Katherine." Even though her sister wouldn't be able to hear her.

A whistle pierced the sky and then a bang had the people on the platform above them scrambling for cover.

Rayne hissed, "Now." Shooting into action they uncovered themselves and she rolled so she was under Victor. His feet finding purchase on her shoulders, she rose a little. He slipped and gagged above her. Eventually he found his footing. He still struggled to breathe above her as the noose had already tightened and didn't easily come loose but he wasn't gagging. She closed her eyes, glad the hangman had a penchant for not setting the knot to break a person's neck. Charles at least had been a font of knowledge on the procedures around executions so she had been sure Victor could heal whatever damage he gained from a hanging.

There were more whistles and bangs and Rayne could see that the crowd had also gone for cover. No one would see that Victor was no longer strangling. His foot slipped again but he caught himself.

Everett cursed and said, "A little higher."

She arched her back, lifting Victor up a little more and taking the tension off the rope.

Everett called, "Now."

She moved, rolling again into the shadows cast under the platform. Victor slipped off her back and slumped into the hole of the trapdoor. Crouching, she rolled Victor who still had the hood and his hands tied, so he was further under the platform. The noose no longer around his throat he could at least breathe easily so she didn't have to worry about him suffocating.

She grabbed the item Katherine had given up for this rescue mission and wedged it under her shoulder. Everett caught hold of it and helped with the dead weight. He slipped the noose over the covered face of the body and then they both dropped down into the trapdoor. The body swung from their manhandling.

Her heart beat so loud that she couldn't hear the fireworks anymore. She rolled further into the shadows and pressed up against Victor's side. She covered the two of them with the black cloth, hiding them from a casual view from above.

Everett crouched in the small space made by the trapdoor. He struck a flint and applied it to the pants leg of the dangling body. A whoosh above them and the heat told her that the body had caught as easily as Katherine had insisted it would. Apparently, many of the chemicals she had used to preserve the body would aid in its combustibleness.

Everett took his own place again under the platform in the shadows. The cries from people were still in fear of the fireworks. None were about their body switching antics.

The fireworks stopped as suddenly as they started. Officials rushed onto the platform but the flames kept them back. The flames finally caught on the rope and the body slammed down onto the platform. Its legs were in the hole but most of it was above them on the slats of the platform.

Rayne gagged at the smell of cooking flesh. She shifted the cover over them more as melted flesh dripped on them through the gaps in the floorboards. A splash of water drenched them more than the body aflame above them.

She tightened her arms around Victor and whispered, "Keep still and quiet." She felt the nod of his head rather than saw it.

The wait was harder than the one before. Bobbies and other officials studied the now charred body, but at least no longer on fire, on the platform.

The officials muttered to themselves. One swore and said, "Freaky dragon stuff."

Another said, "I didn't know they burst into flame when they died."

The first answered, "Who knows. One hasn't died in a long time." As she hoped, they assumed the fire was a dragon thing. She had hoped if they hadn't believed dragons were weird that they would assume whoever had set off the fireworks had also managed to set fire to the body. It was better not to try to anticipate people's conclusions.

The burning had been essential to cover the tattoos and the clear difference in facial features between the dead pirate and Victor. The burnt remains were eventually taken away. The commotion went on longer than she expected even after the body was taken away.

When it was quiet again, she shifted and offered Victor some food. Given permission to move he pulled the hood off his head. He breathed in, taking in fresh gulps. She reached around him and untied his hands.

He ate while her fingers explored the band around his neck that kept him in human form. She couldn't find where it latched. That would have to be a task for Everett and his tools.

Victor said in a whisper, "Thank you."

She patted his arm. They were far from free from this situation. They had to prove Victor was innocent and convict Maynes for the murders before they could have their happily ever after.

Everett passed over some water but she didn't take any. She already needed to go. Everett had produced a jar for Victor but there was no way she would relieve herself while in the small confines with Victor and her brother.

Eventually the sun that had beaten on the wooden boards above them abated and the cool of sunset settled on them.

It was much earlier than expected when Katherine tapped on the side of the platform and opened it up. She looked inside and said, "All clear."

Rayne scrambled out first and rushed to an abandoned alleyway to relieve herself. By the time she returned Katherine was tucking Victor into the cart. Everett rolled up the evidence of their presence under the platform and tucked it in beside Victor.

Kathrine said, "It went swimmingly. Those fireworks really put the fear of dragon into the crowd. No one popped their head higher than a knee while they were going off."

She chuckled as she remembered the whole thing. Rayne was just glad this part was over.

Everett took up the handle of the cart and asked, "Which way?"

Rayne pointed in the direction of Markim's house. She had checked. He didn't have any family, and it would take a while for the lawyers to figure out who owned the house, let alone organise new tenants. It would give them a place to hide while they sorted out this mess. Also, she was hoping to search the place for more evidence.

She placed her hand over Victor's covered form for a moment to remind herself that he was alive. Their small group trudged through the streets. The energy of the day drained out of them in relief.

They slowed as they approached Markim's place as Larkin waited outside of the door. Rayne glanced at Victor's covered form. She didn't want to lie to her partner but she also couldn't tell him what they were up to as it would put his career at risk. Unlike her, he didn't have wealth is fall back on.

Larkin unrolled a newspaper and read the headline, "Lady Golden hand is mated to a Dragon." As a way of greeting, it certainly surprised her. She frowned and he continued with the heading paragraph, "It has come to this writers' attention that the dragon set to be hung this afternoon has found a new bride. None other than Lady Rayne Ancaster. Seen weeping at the trial, a witness has confirmed that her father was in negotiations for her hand with the dragon before..." he stopped reading and raised an eyebrow.

This could complicate things. She had hoped to return home after dropping Victor at Markims. He could recover and fly away. No one would need to know of her part in this situation. There were likely to be someone watching her house and her movements. This forced their hand. If she wanted to go back to her life, she would have to find something to prove Maynes was the real killer.

"I can explain, Larkin." She rubbed a hand over her eyes. Too tired to have any tact, she struggled to find the words to explain anything.

He rolled the paper back up and said, "So is that the dragon under there?"

Rayne's shoulders dropped. Larkin didn't ask for permission but lifted the corner of the cloth covering Victor.

She held her breath, wondering if Larkin would hand them in to the authorities. He wouldn't have to fight them. They would go with him. But she would try to talk him out of it first.

Larkin motioned. "Let's get inside." He glanced around at the neat neighbourhood.

Rayne said, "They didn't hear a very loud murder happen here I doubt they will notice us." It was one of the factors she had taken in when she had picked their hideout. "How did you know we'd be here, Larkin?"

Larkin flashed one of his rare smiles. "I know you, my lady." It warmed her to have all these people in her life who understood her and helped her to achieve what she felt was right in her bones.

Larkin dropped the paper on the table and said, "Lord Rowan gave me a note to pass on to you." Her heart dropped. Charles would not be pleased with what she had done. She knew she was risking her career by saving Victor.

The tone of the greeting on the note though alleviated her fears. He did say she should take a few days off so he couldn't be pleased either.

Rayne glanced at the newspaper and knew why he had suggested it.

Larkin tapped his hat against his hand and said, "I'll pop around some time tomorrow. I'll have a look round to see if I can find anything on Maynes." When Larkin turned to leave Rayne rested her hand on his arm. He turned back with a slight frown.

"Thank you."

He put his hat on and said, "That is what partners are for."

Once he left, she said to Everett and Katherine, "You don't have to stay."

Everett said, "Nonsense. You'll need us to take down Maynes."

Katherine more pragmatic said, "Besides you need a chaperone." She glanced significantly at Victor.

Rayne decided to change the subject and motioned to the collar around Victor's neck that prevented him from changing into his dragon for.

"Let's get that thing off your neck." She hated to see the remnants of his incarceration.

Everett clapped his hands. "Yes, let's see if the blackmailer has any tools."

In the end they used a butter knife and a hairpin to take off the collar around Victor's neck. She watched this from the doorway, worried by Victor's subdued nature. He wasn't a reticent man but he had barely said two words since they rescued him. She wasn't sure it was his near-death experience or the way the people of Londinuim had turned on him. But then it could also be the collar or the fact his own people hadn't been able to bail him out. She supposed he had every right to be quiet but it bothered her, anyway.

CHAPTER TWENTY

Rayne put the chairs, knocked over by the fight that had ended in Markim's death, in their rightful place. The Collectors had cleaned up the blood, leaving a scrubbed area that was significantly cleaner than the area around it. Victor came up next to her and took some candlesticks that had been tossed aside and set them on the mantelpiece.

He asked, "What are you doing up so late?"

The others had gone to bed hours before. She had tried but couldn't sleep. She thought doing something productive would let her mind settle.

She smoothed a hand down her nightgown. Her other hand ended in the stump as she hadn't bothered to put her mechanical hand on to fuss around. She was used to making do, so she hadn't even noticed. Now a little embarrassed she shoved her arm behind her.

Victor stepped forward and slid his hand down her arm, bringing her arm forward. He studied the end. Running his hands over the healed skin.

His voice, holding a touch of awe mixed with curiosity, "Can you feel anything?"

"Of course." In fact, she felt a lot. A shiver ran over her. Victor's eyes came up to her own. His touch becoming reverent rather than curious. Caressing her arm, his thumb a breath over the inside of her elbow. His eyes never left her own. Rayne blushed but didn't pull her arm away.

She saw that there weren't even bruises on his neck from where he had hung. Frowning she said, "You healed very quickly."

He shrugged it off and said, "It's a dragon thing. We can heal almost anything instantly. A little more sophisticated than chemicals but not nearly as fun."

His fingers caressed her skin on her arms as he said in a voice that was deeper than usual, "I haven't thanked you for saving me."

"It was the right thing to do. You didn't hurt those people." She defended him out of habit.

"I have hurt people before. It might be considered justice for my past." He seemed philosophical about his near-death experience.

"Your past?" She knew dragons lived for a very long time so he could be referencing a lot of things.

"I was an angry dragon when I arrived on Earth. The newspapers were accurate."

"That was supposed to be you?" She thought back to the bone-strewn image of a dragon attacking the knight. Victor shifted closer so she could feel the heat coming from his body.

"I wasn't always a nice guy." His voice barely a whisper.

"Are you trying to chase me off?" she asked a little confused by the conversation and her own feelings.

"No, just making sure you know everything before we start anything."

He tipped her head up with the barest tips of his fingers. His eyes sparked with emotion before he lowered his lips to her own. She slipped her arms around his neck. No longer worried what he would think of her lack or that he only liked her because she was unique.

Breathless, he pulled away and muttered, "Why couldn't you choose a room with proper chairs." He glared past her to the single wingback chair.

He bent his knees, taking them both to the floor. Rayne hesitated. She wasn't so sure she wanted to move this fast. But the heat of the moment had her sinking into the feelings and tightening her arms around him.

Victor must have sensed her hesitation as he rolled so she was above him. His hands moving to caress her sides. So she didn't crush him with her weight, she propped herself up with her good hand.

A click had her frowning and glancing up. A small sliver of the floor had lifted. Victor groaned in protest as she pulled away from him. She shifted off him so she could use her good hand to explore the lifted floor panel. It rose easily at her touch as there was a mechanism inside.

She shoved the chairs aside and lifted it completely, revealing a metal-lined case in the floor. Files were neatly stacked on their sides with little tabs showing what each file was about.

She gasped. "He had copies." As she had hoped. What was surprising was how organised he was.

At the end of the files was also a stack of leather-bound books. All bulging with extra pages and kept shut with a strip of leather wrapped around them.

Victor, who had also sat up, muttered, "I see where your true passion lies."

She glanced at him. Blushing at his words. Then she firmed her shoulders. "I did warn you."

He raised an eyebrow. "You did. I apologise. Do you need help?"

She nodded and passed him the first bound journal while she perused the tabs to see if Maynes was mentioned. She was rewarded with a fat folder. Pulling it out from the others she laid it on the floor so she could spread out her find.

Victor took a seat in one of the wing-backed leather chairs and said, "He is very organised. These are his journals dating back to when he first started as a bow street runner."

Without looking up from her own find she asked, "Look for anything about Maynes." He grunted in response at her obvious direction.

She pulled out one page that had a clipping from a newspaper. "It has here an article of when he became one of the leaders of the Yard. It has the same picture I have the plate for."

"Here is a mention of Maynes." Victor cleared his throat before he read, as if he were reading to a child. Putting on a different voice for the narrator. "Don't like the new boss Maynes. He seems too squeaky clean. I don't like it when I don't have leverage. Spoke to his old boss. I like Maynes a little more now. He got passed over for a promotion because of a new law. Dragons meddling again."

Victor looked up and frowned. "I have no idea what law they are talking about. I've had a few changed over the years. I wouldn't know how it impacted anyone. Or really how the law affected Maynes and his promotion but he finally fell in the cream, surely he didn't see a point in holding a grudge against me."

"Ah, but you have to remember all this happened back before his position in the Metropolitan. He might have thought his career was stunted because of that. Is there anything else? Knowing why Maynes might have targeted you is interesting but it isn't going to convince anyone he is a murderer."

He huffed but returned to scanning the pages for any mention of Maynes. Her own attention was already on the files in front of her. There was a letter amongst the other pages that looked like the one that had been burned. The slant of the words were different, so this was a copy. Maynes was the one that had summoned Sebastian.

There were also other notes that Markim had somehow intercepted. They were between Sebastian and Maynes about what they would need to know for Eleanor to seduce Victor. The notes were detailed enough to make her blush.

She asked, "How did Maynes know you?" She held up the page to show the detailed notes of everything that could be of interest about Victor. His eyes snapped with fire, probably at the invasion of privacy or possibly feeling anger at the betrayal all over again.

"He didn't. We only met when he got in the way of me seeing Laurie."

"Do you think he killed Laurie because he asked too many questions about Eleanor?" She was the one to bring up Eleanor to Laurie. "I shouldn't have said anything to him. I'm the reason he is dead."

Victor's voice was fierce, "You didn't hurt anyone. Sir Laurie couldn't have known his friend was a murderer. The only real person to blame is Maynes. He is on a spree, taking out anyone who could know even the least about his crimes."

Rayne sat back on her heels. "I wonder why now? It has been years. He could have left it and no one would have known. It wasn't like Sebastian was making any plans to come here. He hasn't been to Londinium for years."

Victor pointed to another entry in the journal. "This might help. 'I sent the note to Basher. He should be here in a couple of days. I don't bluff.'"

"So Markim had Sebastian come to town and not Maynes. He must have had someone copy his handwriting as Markim's copy is in his own writing."

She smoothed her hands over the different slants of writing in the letters. "Do you think Maynes stopped paying Markim? It would have been expensive to have to pay him for this long. Mmm."

She got thoughtful as she took in all the different pieces if information.

Victor asked, "Is this enough?"

"For Charles? Yes. Whether it will get him convicted is another thing altogether. Maynes has a lot of influence."

Victor interrupted her with an excited, "Ha."

He waved the book and said, "Markim wasn't the only blackmailer. So was Eleanor.

Markim thought it amateurish what she was doing and wasn't surprised it got her killed."

It didn't surprise her that Eleanor blackmailed Maynes. She was an opportunist. It also meant they had to be cautious about taking out Maynes. He tended to kill anyone who went against him.

The panicked nature of Markim's death came back to her. He must have really hated Sebastian to have mutilated his corpse or did he do that purely to get back at Victor. He couldn't have known she would find Markim and make the link between him and the blackmailer.

Markim had a slew of enemies and any one of them could wish him dead. Technically, even Lady Beechworth was on that list. She had known where Markim lived and she had reason to have him silenced. It was the frenzied nature of the attack that pointed to Maynes.

Control, that was the issue she couldn't connect. Maynes liked to have everything under his control. He had all the files in his office until they were no longer relevant. He had everyone file their reports through him. Every word on every report was in his hand. These attacks weren't about control they were about the lack of control.

She sat back on her heels again as she said more to herself to get her thoughts in the right order, "So years ago you got the

Governor to change a law. Because of this Maynes didn't get a promotion and instead went to work for Sir Laurie. There he met Eleanor and Sebastian. He saw what they did to Sir Laurie and decided that you needed the same kind of treatment. So, he contacts them and they like the idea of making as much out of you as they can. You meet them at the inn. They probably had no carriage and just made sure you felt pity for her. That would appeal to your sense of superiority. Coming in to rescue her. I don't think there are many men who wouldn't find that a boost to their pride."

Victor winced. "That doesn't flatter men in general and certainly not me. But I also can't disagree. I liked that I was helping her. Most dragons see it that way. We like to swoop in and be powerful."

"You pitied me for my hand. I knew straight away what kind of person you were. Maynes must have figured that out as well. Or maybe Eleanor and Sebastian, who were already masters at seducing people, figured it out from what Maynes told them."

Victor seemed stuck on what she had first said as he said gently, "I didn't pity you. I thought you were amazing because you are different and you don't let that change who you are."

"But it has. I'm stronger because I haven't had it easy. I shouldn't be pitied though. I have a great family who love me and I have a purpose in life." Her own vehemence surprised her.

Victor put aside the journal and knelt in front of her. He cupped her face. "You are so beautiful right now."

She feared she would end up being a complete watering pot, so she bowed her head, hiding her eyes. She didn't see the kiss coming.

Heat suffused her as she threw herself into the surprising kiss. She screwed her eyes shut as she marvelled in the moment. She could get used to this. But she also feared that it would mean having to make too many sacrifices and she was honestly done with sacrifices. She wanted it all even though she knew sentiment was selfish.

CHAPTER TWENTY-ONE

Rayne looked up from the notes when Katherine found them both lounging in the wing-backed chairs early in the morning. She was bleary-eyed herself and took a moment to take them in.

She frowned and said, "You didn't do anything silly, did you?" Pointing a finger at them each accusingly.

Rayne couldn't help her blush as they had ended up on the floor making out at least once last night. If she hadn't found the hidden cache, they very well could have gone further.

To take away from her embarrassment she made sure her little sister didn't read anything into the blush and insisted, "No, we found Markim's hidden records and journals. He kept copies of everything he used to blackmail people with."

Victor added, "We found out why Sebastian was pardoned."

Katherine raised an eyebrow. Rayne added, "That was all Sir Laurie. He didn't realise that Sebastian was a conman and he felt a little nostalgic and so had him pardoned for Eleanor's sake. Maynes would have preferred that he die and tie up Eleanor's death in a neat bow but his hatred of dragons got the better of him. Maynes, working for Sir Laurie hinted it was the dragon who murdered Eleanor and that tipped Sir Laurie into helping Sebastian. Giving him money and everything. Maynes probably couldn't help himself to dig at Victor. He really did hate dragons."

Katherine asked, "Is there proof here?"

"Several letters. How Markim got hold of them I have no idea. He was certainly good at being a blackmailer." Rayne wasn't sure she should be impressed with his skills but he had been an investigator for the police so maybe he got his skills from that.

Katherine smiled. "Well, bundle up all the evidence. Everett and I will take it over this morning and get everything sorted with Uncle Rowan. Should we tell him about Victor though?"

They might as well come completely clean with him. He knew enough that if he was going to have her fired, he could do that. "Yes. I'm thinking of another approach that if it works should keep him safe from any other attacks from the public as well as Maynes."

Katherine yawned and apologised as she wandered off sleepily to find food for breakfast.

CHAPTER TWENTY-TWO

"Why are we here?" Victor asked. He wore a hat and a scarf though it wasn't really cold enough to be so bundled up. But it would help with people not recognising him.

"Don't you trust Charles?" he accused her.

Rayne pushed open the door to the Times newspaper as she answered, "I trust Charles but we still have to deal with public opinion. Charles won't be able to do anything if everyone thinks Maynes is squeaky clean and that you are the big bad, evil dragon who kills his wife's lover in a jealous rage."

"Don't you think you will be forcing his hand? I've had some experience trying to convince humans to do the right thing. It takes finesse. This is brash and probably foolish."

"I'm untying his hands," She insisted. Victor shrugged. She had carefully picked what she would share with the newspaperman, already aware of what her godfather would be able to do. This was more likely to get results than Charles. He had already admitted to her that because they both held equal positions that even with proof it would be difficult to bring him to justice. Maynes would most likely buy his way out of the charges and it would be reduced to a scandal.

The clacking of the press was loud but the newspaperman wasn't in the press room. They made their way to the back and behind a door where it was much quieter.

They found him working with others to set the type. "Hey, Thomas."

He spun and when he recognised her; he motioned her to the back room where they could close the door and talk without having to yell over the top of the clacking of the press or overheard by his workers.

He wiggled his fingers at Victor and said, "A new chap. This guy a peeler as well?"

She motioned to Victor and he took off his hat and scarf. Thomas gasped as he recognised Victor. "I thought you were dead."

Thomas repeated himself this time softer and to himself. He bounced from foot to foot as he grew excited about the story. He clapped his hands together and asked, "You came to me first, right? This is my present for being such a nice guy before or is it because your dear old daddy likes the paper?"

Her father had discerning tastes but it was clear Thomas was the heart of this paper and if her father thought there was substance to the paper, she would take that as an endorsement. Besides, she had seen the passion Thomas had for his paper and he avoided sensational and inaccurate news.

Thomas didn't wait for her answer and turned to scramble for a piece of paper and ink. His hands fluid as he worked. He ran one hand through his hair too excited to keep still. "Tell it all. How did he do it? Some dragon magic? Is he going to go on another killing spree? Is he in breach of the treaty? Will the other dragons be coming after him?"

He moved things that kept rolling onto the paper. With a frustrated growl he swiped an arm across the surface and knocked off everything except the inkwell and the page he was working on.

Thomas looked up at them when they didn't answer. Victor looked at her. This was her idea, so she was glad he wasn't taking the lead. Besides, he wasn't so sure this was a good idea and had expressed that several times on their way here. She thought it was poetic justice that their problems would be solved by a newspaper. Especially after the trouble they had caused Victor with the news they had been reporting on from Maynes.

Angry at the situation she grabbed Victor's hat and scarf. He gagged as she pulled on the scarf too fast. She placed them on the table now clear of everything but Thomas' notes.

"Victor is innocent. He was framed by the head of the Scotland Yard, Maynes."

Thomas' mouth dropped and he went back to bouncing on his feet. "Even better. Tell it all. Spill."

She told of how Maynes had framed the dragon because of a vendetta and that he had killed Eleanor and Sebastian.

She didn't add in Sir Laurie as she didn't have the evidence for that. She had only extrapolated from what she knew of the crime and his connections to the rest of the events. And she left Markim out as it would only confuse the issue.

It was enough to make Thomas giggle like a schoolgirl as he jotted down notes. She didn't tell him how she had rescued Victor; she let him think it was some power that Victor had managed, despite that his abilities would have been hindered by the collar.

They left without Thomas even realising she had kept things from him. He danced around the back room, his fingers twirling in the air as he came up with headlines for the article he would write.

Outside Victor returned to his cocooned version of himself by wrapping the scarf around the lower half of his face. Donning his hat, he offered his hand. She hesitated.

He asked, "What do you fear?"

"That you will swallow me up whole," she replied honestly.

"You know dragons don't do that anymore."

She shook her head and took his hand. She wasn't about to correct his misconception. She hadn't been talking about the time when dragons ate humans but rather her life and personality. Victor was bigger than life and she was scared she would always be second to the drama that was his life.

CHAPTER TWENTY-THREE

Rayne sorted through the rest of Markim's notes. Placing them into a trunk so they could take the very sensitive documents to the Yard where it could be kept safe. It would take months to contact everyone on the list and inform them of the demise of Markim and their new-found freedom from the blackmailer. She wasn't even sure if they were still paying him and the money collecting in some way. She would have to speak with Lady Beechworth to see if Markim had informed her yet on payment details before she had set her on the blackmailer.

She clicked the trunk closed and sat back on her heels. Victor offered his hand, so she could get to her feet. Once on her feet she dusted off her skirts. Victor ran his hands down her arms and lifted both her hands in his. He studied them both equally. "You know hands are important to dragons. It is how we marry."

"Really?" She didn't pull her hands back, despite where the conversation was going. She wasn't ready for marriage and everything it entailed.

"If a dragon ever asks for your hands, they are actually offering marriage."

"On the spot just like that. No priest? And then bang they are married." If the ton were aware of this, they would be horrified. They loved the ceremony of life, and weddings were a significant event. Usually with an elaborate breakfast and their best clothes. Her mother would insist on a new gown and probably one as revealing as the gold gown she had worn to the ball the other evening. Hopefully, it wouldn't be white like the Empress' gown had been at her wedding. Her statement of a white gown had been important after the previous Emperor's penchant for breaking every vow in his marriage but it wouldn't sit right with Rayne to wear white. Not because she wasn't an innocent but rather she was no naïve chit. She couldn't think of just holding hands being the complete marriage ceremony.

"Yes. We have had some misunderstandings amongst the dragons and humans. We've been told that we have to be clearer when offering." His grin made her think he didn't particularly care that there had been misunderstandings in the past.

She resisted the urge to take her hands back. She wasn't ready for marriage though it wasn't off the books completely like it used to be. Contemplating kissing him she leant forward a little. His eyes brightened with his own desire.

Rayne jumped back when Larkin entered the room accompanied by Charles. She flicked her skirts out in a nervous habit and muttered, "Sir."

Charles motioned for her to take a seat as he took in the room. Victor hadn't completed his reading of Markim's notes in his journal and had that sitting on the arm of the chair. She didn't think there was anything else about Maynes in there but she assumed Victor had been fascinated by some of the things he found about others in society. She worried about what Victor found but she also couldn't think of a reason he shouldn't read it that he would agree with. She just hoped he didn't use anything in there for anything nefarious. But then she was talking about a dragon. He was always up to something.

She waved for Charles to take a seat but he shook his head, "I'm only here to share some news." He didn't sound pleased. But that wasn't a clue about the news he was about to share. Arresting a fellow colleague would not be a time to rejoice for him. "Maynes is in the wind. He didn't come in to work today. We sent people around to his house and it is deserted. There are some signs he has gone to the continent."

Victor snorted and said, "If he is planning to avoid dragons that isn't the best place to go. He should have headed towards the new world. There are very few dragons there." But the continent was also more like England. Many of the people who went on the run did so to places that were familiar to them. Running to a place where you didn't know the rules and the etiquette could be problematic. Besides, there might be people that Maynes knew on the continent who might be able to help him.

It wasn't a very satisfactory ending but it did mean they were safe. Charles added, "Also from what was printed today in the newspapers I don't think he will be returning. Even if the dragons don't find him on the continent. That is the end of this whole situation. So, I expect you back at work on Monday, officer." She bowed her head and Charles returned it before he spun on his heels and left.

Katherine asked, "That is good news, isn't it? You don't have your name smeared because you had a fellow officer arrested. Charles doesn't have to sit through trials and executions. This will be merely gossip and disappear the next time a new scandal appears in the ton."

Rayne pursed her lips. She wasn't so sure, but she wouldn't voice that. Everett got to his feet and clapped his hands to help dispel some of the tension from the room. "Let's head home. I don't know about you but I'm tired of making my own food. I miss cakes."

He didn't wait for an answer before he headed out of the room to pack up their things. Katherine followed. Victor didn't move from his place buried in journals written by Markim and instead asked, "Are you alright?"

"It isn't neat." She wasn't sure what she expected to be the ending but this was not it.

"Life isn't neat," he reassured her with a soft voice. She shrugged and tugged on her skirts as she settled herself.

Victor changed the subject and asked, "Can I come to court you?"

She went still and asked, "I thought you already were."

A grin split his face and he added, "I thought I should make sure you were keen before I continued to pursue you."

"As long as you remember that I'm not going to give up my life in order to be your mate."

"Part of what makes you unique is your work. To take that away from you would lesser your value." She cringed at the thought of dragons and ownership.

She pointed a finger at him and said, "No talk about slavery."

"It isn't." He gave her an innocent grin that told her he would certainly bring up marriage again.

She shook her head and left the room before she got angry at him for insisting that owning didn't also mean slavery.

CHAPTER TWENTY-FOUR

Lady Ancaster called from the foyer, "Don't forget we have that outing later." Rayne still in her nightgown, nodded her head. She would start back at work the next day and Rayne had decided she would spend the day holed up in her own home where she had servants to make her meals and clean up after her. It had been safe at Markim's but it had hardly been homely.

The house was quiet as her father had taken most of the younger ones to the museum. Lady Ancaster was using it as an excuse to do her own exploring and she was going to see the marbles. Too risqué to take children but titillating for herself. She had invited Rayne twice but she had turned her mother down. She couldn't think of anything more awkward than to tour naked statues with her mother.

Rayne had barely turned after her mother had left when the door opened. Turning back, she asked, "Did you forget something…"

Her heart went cold as Maynes pushed his way in with a flintlock aimed at her. She backed up. In her nightgown she was hardly in a position to fight him off. She held up her hands, glad she had bothered to put on her mechanical hand over her gown to see off her mother.

"Easy there Maynes," her voice low and reassuring. The last thing she wanted was for him to panic and shoot her by accident. Dead was dead, accidentally or on purpose made no difference.

His face twisted with anger. Stepping into her foyer, he closed the door without taking his eyes off her. He growled out. "You ruined everything." He motioned with his gun for her to go into the front parlour room.

Keeping her hands where he could see, she backed up into the parlour. Her eyes stayed on the gun. At this range there was no issue of accuracy. If he fired at her she would be dead. He motioned for her to take a seat. She tried to calm him with some words. "We can talk. Try to work things out." It wasn't nearly as effective with the tremble in her voice or with her hands shaking.

"There is nothing to work out. I have a plan." That worried her. Even when he had been panicked and killing in the moment, he had managed to point the murder towards Victor. With him in control and planning he could be very dangerous.

Her knees backed up to the couch and she flopped down. She hadn't wanted to move her hands to catch herself in case he took that to mean she was making a move for a weapon. Not that there was a weapon in the well-appointed room. Her mother might have taught her how to shoot but displaying weapons in the parlour was against her aesthetic. Rayne raised an eyebrow in silent query before she laid her hands in her lap. Maynes glanced over his shoulder.

She asked, "Are you waiting for someone? My family is out for the time being." And she was grateful for that. If her work ever hurt one of her family, it would kill her inside.

"The dragon should be arriving soon," Maynes announced.

"He isn't coming over today. We have a date later this week." She hoped he wasn't on his way but Maynes appeared too smug for it to be a lie.

His lips curled back in a grin that left her cold. "I invited him. This wouldn't work without him." He smirked and that worried her more. She tightened her hand over her metal prosthetic so the shaking wouldn't telegraph her emotions. Rayne knew she had to keep him talking but watching the end of the flintlock wasn't very comforting. The longer she was alive the more options she had.

"I have to ask, Maynes. Why did you have to kill Sir Laurie?"

He snorted. "I suppose it doesn't matter. You are going to be dead soon. He didn't realise that wench was a fraud. I found him drunk at home. He was supposed to be organising funding for my next position."

"Position?" Confused as she didn't realise he would aim for something higher than commander-in-chief at the Yard.

He must have read the confusion on her face as he tipped his head back in a laugh. "Oh, you didn't know? I was going to go into politics. Once again, the dragon gets in the way. I would have been governor last time if he hadn't brought in that law to help workers in factories. I lost a fortune and I could no longer fund my bid for governor. I finally got my feet under me and this happens."

He waved the gun but he realised he was getting emphatic and clicked his tongue. "Clever girl. But I'm set on my course."

He glanced over his shoulder at the knock at the door. He pulled out another gun and called out, "Come in." The door slammed open. Victor rushed in and came to a standstill at the sight of the guns.

He growled deep in his throat. "I'm going to kill you Maynes if you have hurt her."

"I'm fine," she called out. He looked past Maynes to her and took an involuntary step towards her before remembering their circumstances. She winced as she couldn't forget Maynes and his guns.

Maynes motioned with one of his guns for Victor to move. "Over there. Perfect," he announced when Victor started to move.

Victor got halfway across the room before Maynes motioned for him to stop. Anger sparked in Victor's eyes but he stopped in his tracks. Maynes could now keep an eye on both. Guns aimed at their chests.

Victor asked, "What is your plan, Maynes? Kill us both? No one is going to believe that."

Maynes eyes were wild with passion as he spoke. "But they will. You killed your first wife. Why wouldn't they have believed that you killed your second?"

"She has no brands. She isn't my wife," Victor insisted.

"Neither did Eleanor when she died." Maynes was still very smug. His plans were successful so far. Here he had both of them at his mercy.

Victor growled. "She did when she left the house. Was it you who she renounced me to?"

"She did tell me you were a bore. Is that all it takes to get rid of someone like you?" Maynes snorted at the thought. Victor's face was dark but he didn't lay on insults. Rayne was glad he kept Maynes talking. But making him angry wasn't the best way to get out of this situation.

"At least let me say goodbye," Victor said in a defeated voice.

Maynes acquiesced but added sharply, "Quickly."

Victor stepped closer to her and said, "Take my hands."

"No." She knew what he meant to do by taking her hands, it was their ceremony for marriage. The consent of two individuals to be together. And she wasn't ready for that. But she also knew it would give him extra abilities to protect her. Just like with Lala who was as immortal as her husband she had already gathered there was some mystical link between husband and wife for them to share abilities. With her married to Victor he could probably use the same powers he used on himself on her. Maybe even be able to take her from the room like he had done when he had left the ball.

He gave her a significant look and said, "Then take mine." He was offering himself to her rather than the other way. She wasn't any more pleased with this turn of events. People shouldn't own others.

She hesitated. She knew why he wanted to do it. Maynes got testy and hissed, "I don't have all day. There is a schooner waiting for me and I will not miss it because you two lovebirds have some cryptic goodbye to enact."

Victor gave her a significant look. She said, "I'm going to undo this as soon as I can."

"I wouldn't expect anything less." She took the hands he offered.

When nothing happened straight away, she asked, "Victor?"

"Wait. I hear it takes time and commitment if there is a limb missing." Her heart dropped. Because she had a metal hand instead of a real hand, there was a chance this magic of dragons wouldn't work. Or was it because she didn't really want to be married. This was her fault. Her fault that Maynes was free and not sitting in a jail. It was her fault for this magic not to work because she was less than most people. She looked over Victor's shoulder to Maynes. If she pulled Victor forward and twisted him around the bullets would hit her instead of him.

Before she could make any more plans to maybe throw herself at Maynes and try to fight him for the gun, pain ran up her arms. Brands etched in delicate curls and patterns to show a scene of two dragons wrapped around each other. There was a screech as the brand covered her metal hand as well.

Maynes gasped. "What is this?" He got nervous and pulled the trigger on his flintlock. The bullet hit her shoulder, knocking her back. But Victor was still holding her and twisted her around and away from Maynes.

Maynes pulled the trigger on his second flintlock. Victor jerked as the bullet hit him. But she wasn't too worried as dragons were notoriously robust creatures. If Fields had believed only a gun able to take down elephants was capable of killing a dragon then a flintlock was barely a risk.

Victor's eyes still held life as he looked down at her. He lay a hand over her shoulder where she had been hit and the wound no longer pained her.

There was then a blue flash. Her stomach fell out from under her as she went from being in the world to being somewhere completely different. Air was ripped out of her lungs. It was a moment before she was standing behind Maynes. She gasped for breath which hitched and burned its way back into her lungs.

Victor gave her a look, asking silently if she was alright. She nodded though she could see the pain in his own eyes from his own wound.

Maynes spun but Victor was already moving. Knocking the one flintlock out of his hand and slamming his hand into Mayne's face. Maynes cried out with pain, stumbling back.

He pulled another flintlock and shot blindly. The bullet pinged as it ricocheted off her hand. That got her moving. Not willing to further damage her hand by using it to punch someone, she grabbed a vase off a side table and smashed it over Maynes' head.

Victor grabbed the now stunned Maynes and slammed his head into his knee. Maynes collapsed backwards, unconscious. Victor stumbled back and with a groan went to one knee.

She asked concerned, "Victor?"

He held up a hand. "In a moment." The blood that had run down his back stopped flowing. She shifted the cloth aside where the bullet had pierced the cloth and made a hole. The wound was pink with a healing scar.

She asked, "The bullet?"

"Dissolved. Same as your own." She helped him to his feet as he was still a bit wobbly.

She said with some awe in her voice, "That is one neat trick." He caught her mechanical hand. There was a dent where the bullet had ricocheted. He frowned and rubbed it with his thumb. The plate popped as it returned to its flattened form.

"Mmm. I didn't know it would do that," he said with a frown creasing his forehead.

"Do what?" Rayne asked.

He looked into her eyes. "It is harder to manipulate metal. I shouldn't be able to fix your hand so easily." He turned it over to show the etched brand on the metal. He pushed up her sleeve to where the mechanical hand joined with her skin. The brand moved seamlessly from her skin to the metal.

"It really is a part of you. That is the only answer."

"The brands saved my life." Or at least a long time of recovery from the bullet wound in her shoulder. There was a tense silence.

Maynes groaned and they realised that everything wasn't finished. A curtain sash became a rope to tie up the disgraced peeler. He didn't come to right away but groaned a little more as they moved his arms into a position so they could tie him up.

Victor said, "You know you can break the bond now if you want."

"Later. Let's get this cad in gaol and then we can tie up loose ends."

CHAPTER TWENTY-FIVE

Larkin hung the frame on the wall. He stepped back to admire his handy work. Rayne was reading through the letters that had arrived on her desk. All addressed to Lady Golden Hand. Some gushed over how amazing they thought she was. While others asked for her to talk on their behalf with Victor. There were the occasional one that vilified her as a demon for daring to do anything besides marry and have children but those all ended in the bin beside her.

Larkin said, "He did a good job." She looked up at the article he had framed. It was one from the Times and written by Thomas Barnes. The heading announced that Lady Golden Hand had taken down a rotten peeler. She didn't like the title but she was getting used to the name. At least with the commoners they didn't mean the name ironically and instead spoke it with reverence. She still wasn't sure what to do with that. At least Thomas had made it impossible for the government to use her as a scapegoat for Maynes' misdeeds.

The execution had taken place yesterday. This time it hadn't been public. Charles Rowan had decided the quieter it happened the better. Hopefully, the newspapers would find some other story and society would titter over another scandal.

Fields interrupted by rapping his knuckles on the doorframe. He had taken Mayne's position though he wasn't pleased about it.

Throwing a folder on the desk he said, "You are going to be writing up your own reports from now on Ancaster." He nodded to Larkin and left.

Rayne let out the breath she had been holding and when Larkin raised an eyebrow she said, "What? I was worried he was going to yell at me."

"He likes you." The smile on his lips also evident in his voice.

She snorted at the idea and picked up the folder. It was the notes on Sebastian's case. It was woefully incomplete because the last time she had updated it with Maynes was after she had discovered who the ring had belonged to. There had been several other murders and the conclusion of Maynes trial to put into the notes.

Larkin sat down. "I'm serious. He treats all of us like that." She would believe him when she saw it for herself. She was grateful that Larkin would still be working with her and could play interference with Fields if she needed it.

Another knock on the doorframe had them both looking up. Victor leaned on the doorframe. Larkin coughed and said, "I'm going to get some tea. You want any?" She nodded and he slipped past Victor.

Victor waited until he was sure that Larkin wouldn't overhear him when he said, "I'm still branded."

"Mmm, I know." She shuffled the papers aside so she could bring her attention to Victor.

"I thought you were going to divorce me." He settled on the edge of the desk.

"I'm still thinking about it." He glanced through the doorway to make sure there weren't any other peelers close by before he closed the gap between them.

He caught up her hands. Kissing the knuckles of both. "Take your time."

His eyes hot.

He dropped her hands with a light caress. "Also, I came in to tell you I have a new job."

She caressed her hand over his arm and asked, "Mmm, and what is that?"

"I'm going to be the forensic scientist for the Yard. Charles has set me up a laboratory here in the building. I'll be able to see you every day."

She frowned and asked, "Is that even a position. I didn't know we hired scientists."

His grin reminded her that he liked to tease. "Oh, they do now."

He must have made a deal with Uncle Charles to get this position. She pulled back a little and said, "You can't interfere with my work."

His voice a purr, "I wouldn't dream of it."

When he went to leave, she tightened her hands on his and tugged so he would come close again. He flashed a grin that was hotter than expected as he leant down and kissed her. Sitting back on her desk, he eventually broke the kiss. She was flushed as she let go of his hands. He blew her a kiss as he left her office.

She shook her head and went back to her letters. This one wasn't addressed to Lady Golden Hand but instead to herself. Frowning she opened it. It was from her brother. She hadn't seen him this morning when she had left for work but that wasn't unusual. Her parents' house in Londinium was large. Everett liked to sleep in and she started early. She bit her lip as she read the letter.

Dear Rayne,
My favourite sister. You are probably wondering why I'm writing a letter when I could just find you after dinner or over breakfast but while you are reading this I am on a ship to the continent. I'm going to learn

from Jasmine how to make limbs like your own. Just like you, I'm tired of not having a purpose, so I am going to find one. Please tell the parents. I couldn't tell them to their face as I was worried mother would somehow make me change my mind.
Love Everett

She had to smile over the last line. He must remember the arguments her mother and Rayne had when she had decided to be a police officer. One thing about her mother. Once she had made up her mind her mother had supported her all the way. Closing the letter, she placed it back into the envelope. She put in her desk away from the slew of letters from newfound fanatics. Her parents would ask about it but it was better if they didn't see it. Her mother would be hurt to think he hadn't said goodbye properly because of her but she would get over it.

About the Author

Nix Whittaker is a high school teacher in a small rural town tucked away in the middle of the North Island of New Zealand. She immigrated to New Zealand, when she was a young girl, from South Africa and has completely embraced the New Zealand lifestyle.

She has been writing from a young age when she read all the books available for people her age and was forced to write her own just to feed her voracious appetite for Literature.

She got into reading as she had dyslexia and the teacher thought reading would improve her spelling. Frankly, it never did, but it did lead her to a passion for the written word.

She studied at Auckland University, but opted for the quiet life in the rolling countryside and views of Tongariro National Park. She lives with her dog and her three cats and writes between planning lessons and socializing with friends.

You can contact her at
Reshwity@gmail.com
Or at her website www.nixwhittaker.com

Thank you

Thank you for reading the third book in my glyph warrior series. I would really, really appreciate it if you left a review. Yes, I am begging. Reviews can make or break an author so please review this book. Also if you sign up at my website then you can go in to win prizes, like free books and other prizes.

Thank you again for reading my book and I hoped you enjoyed it.

Other books by Nix Whittaker

Wyvern Chronicles
The Blazing Blunderbuss
The Mechanicals
Wyvern's Trim and other stories
The Jade Dragon
Ruby Beyond Compare

Softcover, ISBN 978-0-473-46823-1
Epub, ISBN 978-0-473-46824-8